Unnatural Truth

CHRISTOPHER HAWKE

ISBN: 0615475957
ISBN-13: 978-0615475950

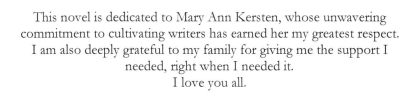
This novel is dedicated to Mary Ann Kersten, whose unwavering commitment to cultivating writers has earned her my greatest respect. I am also deeply grateful to my family for giving me the support I needed, right when I needed it.

I love you all.

CONTENTS

ACKNOWLEDGMENTS

Thanks to all of you in Mary Ann's Rocky Mountain Fiction Writers group who helped me "dot my i's" and breathe life into my characters. Special thanks to Ed Hickok, my friend and fellow author who never abandons his dreams. Also, thank you Shana, for being a creative consultant and a wellspring of inspiration.
Without all of you, *Unnatural Truth* would not have been written.

1 THE DRAGON'S CURSE

Reality lived on my uncle's farm.

I saw it firsthand among rustling corn fields when I visited with my family. I felt like a farmer in my blue-jean overalls, though I was barely old enough to go for walks alone.

The cool morning air left fading ghosts of breath.

I struggled my way inside enormous barn doors and heard the fatal screams of livestock. Blood, dung and hay mixed a scent, as ancient as the first animals.

A child doesn't know to flee from such things, so I crept in, pausing at the first dying cow. Its wholesome eyes were the diameter of cream saucers. Its udder ballooned with milk.

I wanted to help her in any way possible, not realizing possibilities are more easily seen than caught. I stroked above the ribbons of flesh torn in her bleeding neck. Her brown eyes sought me out. She hadn't surrendered.

A wolfish cry trembled from deep in the barn, followed by a pitiful moan.

My father entered and swept me away.

* * *

Whenever I asked about that day, my parents' answer was always the same: a dragon had come and killed the animals. I envisioned a red beast gorging itself with blood-soaked meats.

We never visited my uncle or his family again. Eventually, I learned that he was the mad beast who had destroyed his animals and farm.

"That farm was his life," my mother once said. I think she was right. Sometimes people kill themselves in unconventional ways.

I wondered what he saw when he looked into the mirror—a man or something else. I peer into my own telling reflection. Unlike the eyes of the dying Holstein, my eyes are deep-sea green, but somehow hold the same meaning. I've been hurt, but I have not given up.

* * *

My father got me a job at a meat-packing plant many years later. Each day I'd go home with smears of blood tracking the front of my uniform. It was a horrible three weeks.

I answered a job posting at the plant and escaped from the slaughter floor to an office with a man named Jack Carris.

Jack came with the office, which made sense because he looked like the office, small with an old-fashioned decor. He actually enjoyed coming in on cold mornings with a steaming cup of coffee and a sporty tie. We were the data-entry department.

As calendars were replaced, I forgot what other parts of the company looked like. On an average day, within half an hour of waking I'd shower, dress, kiss my wife, Jane, five-year-old daughter, Ashley, and be on my way to work.

Each day, I entered hundreds of invoices into the mainframe. Jack and I would talk about the weather, my most recent fight with Jane, and the juicy bits of company politics on the vine that day.

Sometime between five and six, I'd make my way back to Golden Acres to spend my final waking hours with my family. These were not bad years, simply years I barely remember, nestled between the birth of my daughter and the insanity of today.

* * *

Waking Monday morning, I tried not to think about the week ahead. Life had become like a picture hanging in your house, one you no longer see.

Thinking back, I don't remember the day being any different from the hundreds of weekdays preceding it. It was unpleasantly warm, I do remember that, and Jack wasn't at Spencer Meats. It wasn't like him not to leave a message.

I asked Bridget, a sandy-blond who worked in Human Resources whether Jack had called in. She laughed and asked me what I was talking about.

I said, "Jack Carris, the man who works with me on the second floor."

She looked through a file cabinet with as many files as the company had employees. Jack had no file; there was nothing between the names Brooke and Carstair.

I thought she was joking. I thought everyone was joking, claiming not to remember Jack. Even those who'd talked with him the day before he disappeared claimed not to remember him.

I spent the afternoon in our office watching a ticking wall clock consume minutes. Jack's desk lay bare—stripped of the stacks of paper that once covered it.

I was alone. It gave me time to generate theories on what might have happened. I wondered if he'd gotten fired doing something not even gossips in the office would repeat. I wondered if he'd asked to be transferred to another plant. His disappearance haunted me.

* * *

Jane and I were married four years earlier on July 20th. She was stunning when we first met, even in her lime-green King Foods' cashier's outfit. Sometime between the pack of taco shells and the ground sirloin, it was love at first sight—at least for me. For her it took another twelve trips. I bought so much food during our courtship that unpacked canned goods lined the entry hall of my home.

A week ago, Jane and I splurged on fireworks for July Fourth. Our friends Jacob and Mary brought over their infant son, Max, and helped us celebrate.

Jacob and I had known each other for years, my only friend from my three-week tour of duty on the slaughter floor.

The fireworks were the best any of us had seen. Raspberry, blueberry and lemon-yellow sparks sprayed and rained onto the street in front of our house.

Jane held Ashley's hand. Flavored light danced on their faces.

They were both immortalized for me that night, with natural smiles and wet-crystal eyes—snapshots to keep in my memory.

"You look beautiful," I shouted above the concussion.

Jane mouthed the words, "Yes, they are."

Jacob, Mary and Max watched, posed as if in a family photo.

Ashley tugged at my leg. "Can I light another one?"

I leaned down and handed her a box of matches. "Be careful."

There's no greater joy than celebrating freedom as young parents. Our children's faces shone brighter than the colored storm.

* * *

Two days passed.

It was late; moths circled and leapt, fighting for the best spot at the porch light. The sky threatened rain with distant peals of thunder. I unlocked the door, with one hand going into my pocket for change. It was a bit of a bribe, but made Ashley happy and brightened my mood each night I saw her.

A child has the power to transform adults into batteries; they are able to charge or drain us at their whim. Ashley charged me every evening I opened the door. Many times, I drove home feeling as if I were approaching a suburban tomb. Ashley had the power to rejuvenate me with the thankfulness on her face. However, there was no charge that night, and I've felt drained ever since.

A TV news station ranted about a string of unsolved murders in nearby Charlottesville.

I snuck into the family room hoping to surprise my daughter, but the green, flower-patterned sofa sat empty. The kitchen was also bare. An unstirred soufflé, tilled by a whisk, sat in a bowl on the countertop.

Something must have been urgent. There wasn't a note. Perhaps Jane or Ashley was hurt. I called friends. Jane hadn't contacted Mary and Jacob, or anyone else we knew. No hospital had anyone with their names being treated. So, I spent hours driving in the rain looking for my family.

Jacob arrived later that night and drove me to the police department to file a missing persons report. I feared the worst. I'd never cried in front of Jacob before, but while riding to the station in his truck that night, my emotional dam burst.

My wife, my dearest companion, and my beautiful, innocent daughter had been kidnapped, stolen out of our home. I was sure of it and had no idea what to do.

Jacob drove without looking over. Snot ran down the stubble on my chin. He didn't offer Kleenex or tell me it was going to be all right. Jacob was a true friend.

"Did you guys have a fight or anything?" he asked.

I shook my head and looked at the puddles on the side of the road. Street lights reflected from them like underwater lanterns. The truck shattered the images.

I searched my mind for where Jane might have gone.

Jacob parked his truck among squad cars.

Inside, I was brought back to my senses by a man yelling. "I'm telling you, he's driving back and forth in front of my house. He's threatening my wife. If you don't do something this time, I will."

Two officers, who looked as if they were hiding tires under their blue uniforms, took him to a small office nearby to file a report. I overheard one of them say, "Of course the guy's driving in front of his house. He lives next door!"

They laughed.

I was beginning to feel stupid. I called home and let the phone ring. It kept ringing.

A cop in her late thirties stood behind the counter. She was busting out of the seams of her uniform. The skin under her chin reminded me of the wattle of turkeys searching for dried corn on my uncle's farm.

She licked her fingers and flipped pages on a clipboard. "Can I help you?"

"Yes. I came home tonight and my wife and daughter weren't there."

She stared, blankly.

"It's not like her to leave without a note or something," I continued.

"Any sign someone forced entry to the house?"

"I don't think so."

"They'll have to be missing for at least twenty-four hours before we can do anything."

My heart sank. She gave me a business card and told me to call if they weren't home by morning. She told me most people that go missing show up within hours of the first report.

We drove back to Golden Acres. Jacob offered to stay until Jane returned, but I told him to go home. At that point, I still thought that things would be okay. I've never been so wrong.

"You know how women are," said Jacob, leaving. "She'll show up."

I watched the eleven o'clock news, half hoping to hear something about a kidnapping or a hostage situation. I grabbed a beer from the fridge and noticed the mixing bowl—once full of tonight's dinner—contained only remnants of batter. The bowl squeaked when I ran my finger against its porcelain bottom. It had been full of an uncooked soufflé.

I turned on every light in the house and called out my daughter's and wife's names. I expected to find them hiding in a closet or laughing behind the blue-and-white-striped shower curtain, but there was no answer. I sat on the edge of the tub, next to the Burt and Ernie bubble bath and Ashley's washcloth and wept.

I trudged back to the kitchen and examined the egg-like film left in the bowl. I wondered if I was stumbling down the same path my uncle had gotten lost on. Someone was fucking with me, or I was farther down that road than I knew. Somehow, I was in the barn again, the dragon breathing on my neck.

I slammed a container of sugar against the wall over the stove. Grains spilled. I tore out a drawer and chucked it at the floor. A rampage ensued.

2 PARTIAL ADMISSION

He sits in a black leather chair, behind a desk you'd expect a psychologist to have. The plain, white wall behind him is checkered with awards and diplomas noting the outstanding accomplishments of his plain, white life. The room smells of cowhide and sorrow.

Dr. Matthew Sherman is a pencil of a man, with puffy lips that look both painted and injected with collagen. In Los Angeles, thin-lipped models would have flocked to ask him who'd done such fine work, but in Wakefield, Virginia, he looked like a hundred-and-twenty-pound perch.

I sit in one of the chairs—specially crafted for emotional outpouring—and share the last six days. "Life's the same. I go to work, do my job and go home. When I get home, my wife and daughter aren't there. So, I usually end up drinking and watching TV for the rest of the night. I've called everyone. No one's heard from her. I visited eleven or twelve hospitals. The police are no help."

Dr. Sherman straightened his tie and set his notepad on the desk. "Did your time off from work help?"

I nodded.

"Where did you go?"

"Lots of places . . . Alaska."

"Alaska! You drove to Alaska?" Matthew shook his head in disbelief.

"I did a lot of thinking," I said. "It's not easy working for a company where everyone thinks you're out of your mind."

"I've been checking into the disappearance Jack Carris at Spencer Meats. They have no record of him ever working there."

"I know. Everyone's acting like he never existed."

Matthew looked as if he were carefully picking sentences out of a list in his head. "Why do you think Spencer Meats has no record of a Jack Carris?"

I shrugged.

"I think you know."

"You've got to believe me. Jack is as real as you or me. I worked with the man for *five* years. There are people there who know him better than I do."

"Have you spoken to these people recently?"

"Yes."

"And what do they say?"

"They deny ever knowing him, just like everyone else does. They act like he never existed, like I'm out of my mind."

"And why do you think they would do that?"

"I don't know. Maybe they killed him. Maybe they're all in on it."

"Does that seem logical to you, everyone at Spencer Meats covering up a murder?"

"No, but nothing's logical right now."

Tears welled from a place so deep I had no idea it existed. Salty water rose to the surface from a spiral staircase within my heart.

"Are you trying to tell me my family never existed?"

Matthew didn't answer right away. He looked at me with a well-paid expression of care. "I'm not saying that, but if you're saying that, we can talk about it."

Inside, I stood naked on a battlefield between rival medieval armies, contemplating the things Matthew suggested.

* * *

Since Jane and Ashley's disappearance, I'd slept on the couch in the family room and fallen asleep to the glaring face of David Letterman, washed over by waves of canned laughter.

That night, I lay in my own bed and stared at the ceiling. It was here Jane and I had made love and shared our plans for the future.

What Matthew suggested was impossible. There was no way my family was a psychotic delusion. I pondered the relation between the disappearances of both Jack Carris and my family.

* * *

Jacob and I drove to Charlottesville on Friday night. I'd hoped to escape my troubles. They followed me, like a tin can tied to my leg, clinking when I walked.

The young were out, imprinting the world with their ways. Dating, walking hand in hand, cruising the strip with beefed-up cars no parent could dream of affording. The engines sounded like hungry, mechanical tigers. I grew faint in the exhaust fumes.

The night was alive and advancing toward a time when inhibitions and other sacred things would be lost.

We strolled near the university where nightclubs lined the streets. People chatted about their lives, never questioning their meaning. They shared time with each other without realizing the gift of their togetherness.

I would have given anything to spend a night like that with Jane and tell her I love her.

The street was jammed with cars moving at half-speed. The sidewalk teemed with folks laughing and enjoying themselves.

Jacob and I treated ourselves to double scoops of chocolate banana crunch ice cream. I swallowed every yellow chunk with guilt.

Couples surrounded us, each sitting at their own ornate iron table with its own Bud Light umbrella. A few fierce stars defied the city lights and speckled the heavens.

Jacob spooned frozen banana into his mouth. "Glad to be out?"

"Yeah, it's been a while. It's good to be in the city again."

A horn honked. Someone shouted in the distance.

Jacob's thin-fingered hand gripped my shoulder. "I'm sorry. I can't imagine what you're going through. If there's anything I can do, let me know."

I noticed a wadded napkin on the table—its edges caught the breeze. One gust and it would drop onto the ground and be forgotten. "You've helped so much already. Thanks for being here for me."

Across the street, people dined at a patio restaurant, stabbing their knives and forks into expensive dishes under a canopy of burgundy umbrellas. Glass oil lamps burned—their flames swaying in the air.

The place reminded me of something holy, like the front of an *Our Lady*, only the figure of Christ had been replaced by a marble sculpture of a woman riding a fish. Instead of priests, waiters in white aprons served bread and wine.

My eyes opened wide. Jane sat leisurely, sipping. I couldn't believe it. I jumped to my feet and ran across the road, amazed and horrified, overjoyed and concerned. The diners watched.

I hit the railing hard with a pang. "Jane, Jane!"

My wife and the man with her turned toward me.

"Do I know you?" she asked.

"Do you know me? Of course you know me. We're married. Where's Ashley?"

I wish I could forget the expression. I wish I didn't remember her that way. Curiosity turned to fear. The man at the table rose from his chair—a bear in a cashmere sweater. I could care less. I'd found my wife.

He leaned over the rail. "You need to leave."

Jane pushed her chair back from the table.

"Not without my wife."

"You're deranged, man! We've been married for years. Get out of here."

"Jane," I pleaded.

"My name's not Jane," she said.

"Yes it is!"

The circus bear grabbed my neck as he crossed the fence and led me away from the patio. He was strong, but weaker than his size. A well-placed elbow freed me.

I ran back to my wife and was tackled. The weight of the animal pressed my cheek into the pavement. My chest collapsed beneath me, as he pressed his knee into my back.

Jacob grabbed the man from behind and slowly pulled him off me, careful of his flailing arms.

The police arrived, cuffed us and pushed us into their black-and-white cars. My wife had her head in her hands and was leaning against the man who had road-rashed my face.

We were taken though swinging doors into the back of the police station. I was frisked, touched in places no man had ever touched me.

* * *

I once held a belief that life made sense, that working toward a dream would birth substance. Nothing else mattered. I soon discovered that success is as long-lasting as any of life's novelties.

We've all been happy with new things, only to be disappointed later. Dolls and soldiers our parents toiled to give us found their way to pedestals, then to the back of closets.

I'd always dreamed of marrying a woman I loved and watching my children grow. I wonder if our lives should be filled with the pursuit of such dreams, those magical hopes interwoven into our story. Our stories are decorative shells for the crabs we really are, both protecting and exposing us to the manic outside.

* * *

Mary bailed us out. Jacob told me the woman only looked like Jane. I realized my problems existed inside, as well as outside, of me.

3 INTO THE SHADOWS

I was dropped off in front of my house and collapsed into bed, near dawn.

My bedroom appeared larger than normal. The walls seemed unreachable; the bed, land, surrounded by oceans of carpet. Jane's perfume tinged the air with memories and sadness. I imagined Jane and Ashley laughing in the family room. I wanted nothing more than to be with them, the way I was when I took them for granted.

A grim, emaciated silhouette appeared out of the corner of my eye. It advanced from the doorway, dragging a dead leg. Shadows ascended the walls. My heart climbed from the comfort of my soul.

The form's misshapen head shuddered atop a warped body, jerking as though attempting to escape its neck. Its snake-like limbs quivered.

I froze.

I couldn't run. My body shook.

A putrid smell slapped my face. The beast watched, as though it derived pleasure from my fear. It slowly backed away, until engulfed by the darkness of the hall.

I leapt to my feet, feeling as though I were in my own grave. I turned and expected to see my corpse lying limp on the bed, but saw only sheets and pillows. The door and hall looked like a surreal painting.

I grabbed a knife from the nightstand drawer and edged my way out the door. The hall seemed a mile long. My legs trembled and threatened to give out. I snapped on a lamp. Light and dark fought for life in the living room.

I thought about dialing 911, but instead turned on every light. Around every corner, I expected to be mauled; in every room, torn apart. Every square foot searched led me closer to my own insanity.

The next day, I asked Matthew to help commit me.

* * *

Defects in the structure of my nervous system are leading to abnormal behavior. I learned this in a large, pale-yellow room that smelled like Thanksgiving dinner and vomit. We sat in a circle of maroon folding chairs—the kind churches use for potlucks. We faced each other, knowing the secret everyone else there knew: half our lives had been wasted imagining shit.

We're the schizophrenics. Our homes are concrete cells with steel doors that lock from the outside.

Because I committed myself, I get to stay in an area with much less screaming than the rooms down the hall.

We're free to play board games in the activity room or stroll around the lake. We're free to read, nap or chat. We're free to learn.

But we're not free.

Many of us aren't sure what's worth remembering, and scared of learning something that might devastate our shared reality—a life of medication, psychotherapy, barbed-wire fences and long suffocating halls lined with doors.

* * *

On my first day, I walked around the lake. A man lapped me twice with a steady stride. His arm was bandaged tight to his chest.

"He's a power walker," said someone from over my shoulder. She was trying to keep up with the man, without much luck. Her squirrel-cheeked, freckled face exuded both cheer and sadness. Hazelnut hair dangled in curls just shy of her shoulders and lively breasts.

"I keep trying to walk with him, but he's just too fast." She extended her hand. "I'm Rhonda."

"Brendan."

"You must be new."

I nodded. "Yeah."

"Sorry."

"For what?"

"If you don't know, I guess that's why they locked you up."

"Why are you in here?"

"Chemical imbalance," she said, tapping the side of her head with her finger.

"Same with me . . . I guess. How long have you been here?"

"Almost three years."

"I can't imagine being here that long."

"Hopefully, you won't be. They only make you stay if you're not improving."

"And you're not?"

"I haven't yet." She looked into my eyes for the first time.

Rhonda is a sad woman, or ecstatic, depending on the day, the hour or the alignment of the planets. We walked and talked. She told me about the time she saw Fidel Castro in a coffee shop, and I told her about my missing family. She said,

"It wasn't really Fidel, but that didn't keep me from bitching him out for being a Communist pig."

Similar outbursts landed her in Saint Thomas's Sanitarium. Her husband convinced her to commit herself and then ran off to Florida with one of her friends. Rhonda doesn't get better because she has no reason to. I wonder what reason I have.

* * *

I lay in my new bed later that night. It sagged in the middle like a foam-filled hammock and smelled of urine and Lysol. There was nothing to do but be within myself and feel. My soul drowned in a flood of loneliness. The waters overtook me. I rested with nowhere to flee and listened to the reverberating sounds of terrified people down the hall.

Even here, the nightmare figure crept into sight—nude and grotesque. Layers of crusty filth covered its lanky form. Dark, blank eyes shone with horror. It returned from a pure black hole that had materialized in the corner of the room.

I screeched, curled into a ball and wept. "Leave me alone."

The creature sneered.

I rocked myself, eyes closed, expecting its icy touch. When I opened my eyes, it was gone.

I wrestled with sleep and the idea that my monster seemed as real as my family.

* * *

A storm brewed. Muddy clouds stirred, as though the hospital was scum at the bottom of god-sized caldron. Lightning flowered in the distance.

Rhonda heard about the encounter on our daily walk around the lake.

"Until now, you seemed sane," she said. "I was beginning to wonder why you were in here."

I noticed that Rhonda wasn't wearing any shoes. Her bare, white feet clumped before her like a pair of oversized boots.

"It seemed so real," I said.

"If it didn't," said Rhonda, "you wouldn't be loco. Time to up the meds. If you play it right, you can get just about anything you want in this place."

"What happened to your shoes?"

Rhonda pointed at me emphatically. "Indians!"

"What about them?"

"I'm reading a book. Gurus go around barefoot."

"You're not a guru," I said.

"No." She looked at her trotting steps. "That guy Randy has had a hurt back for the last four weeks. Before that, it was his hip or something. He's always got a butt-load of pills."

I pressed on my lower back with the palm of my hand. "If they don't give me a different mattress, I don't think I'm going to have to fake it."

Rhonda smiled, exposing a chipped tooth.

I remembered Ashley's giggle. I thought of Jane's face last Christmas when I got her real silverware and china plates. I wondered if a smile was the first thing happiness invented.

Misfortune runs rampant early in our lives. If we were wiser, we would welcome it as an indicator of hope. Instead, we learned to hide from disappointment, no matter the cost. The hospital's corridors are lined with people who no longer smile or laugh, those held in constant disenchantment by the all-encompassing details of life.

* * *

Dr. Blake, a balding man with an upturned nose, wearing a red-and-blue, geometrically patterned sweater, led a session in the folding-chair circle. Rain streamed down the lines of paned windows high above and pelted the roof with a subtle roar.

The doctor scanned our faces looking for a target. "Who thinks they see reality clearly?"

Several hands shot up.

"And what about the rest of you? What's most unclear right now? Jake, what about you?" he asked, looking at a large black man in a baby-blue jumpsuit.

Jake's eyes gleamed, red and wet.

"It happened again, Dr. Blake. I didn't mean no harm by it." Tears fell from the muscular man.

Rhonda and I looked at each other from across the circle. It was always something. Jake masturbates uncontrollably. He kills whatever animal he gets his hands on and stores carcasses in various hiding places. Every other week, a rancid smell emanates from his room, and the staff goes on a bizarre scavenger hunt.

Dr. Blake spent some time straightening Jake out. He said just the right words to get Jake through the next six hours of his tortured life, before another mishap toppled its supports and it fell again into melancholy pieces.

I watched the windows high above and noticed that water never streamed down the panes the same way twice. The drops took new and different paths, but ended up in the same place, as we all had.

"How are you today, Brendan?" asked the doctor.

I glanced his way, then down at the floor.

I had no idea. I didn't know if what I saw that morning was real. I didn't even know how much of my life had been real. "Fine," I said.

"So why didn't you raise your hand a minute ago?"

Whenever Rhonda was made to share, she somehow ended up on the subject of world politics. I had nothing so distracting to fall back on.

The words slipped from my mouth. "Something climbed out of the floor in my room last night." The words seemed right, but I was struck by how crazy they made me seem.

"What was in your room, Brendan?"

"I don't know."

"What did it look like?"

"A demon."

Dr. Blake scribbled something onto his notepad.

* * *

Jacob visited a week later. I was beside myself, showing him my new home.

"So how are things at the plant?" I asked as we entered the game room.

"Oh, you know, you're missed."

"Sure I am."

"We had a huge load of Angus this month, close to two-thousand head."

An elderly albino woman fought with puzzle pieces on the table next to us. Next to her, two men wearing bathrobes and slippers played chess. A wrinkled, former debutante sat on a couch against the farthest wall, her left breast exposed.

Jacob folded his arms. "So how are you getting along?"

"I've been better."

"Understandable."

"Things are confusing. Do I have a family? Did you drive me to the police station?"

"Of course you have a family. I still haven't heard from the police. I'm waiting for their call, like you asked."

"I still see that thing. It won't leave. The drugs make me tired, but they don't help my hallucinations."

"That's horrible."

"That's why I asked if I have a family. I'm so fucked up right now, I don't even know myself."

"If my wife and daughter disappeared, I'd need a sanity check, too. You're going to be all right."

"Am I going to be all right without my family?"

Jacob took a deep breath and looked at the albino jamming puzzle pieces into place.

* * *

Two weeks passed. That meant fourteen walks with Rhonda, exploring life and reality. It meant listening to patients explain over and over how their symptoms are caused by a disease they will somehow conquer, how they're going to get better one day and go back to their warm, comfortable homes. It's sad. It's as crazy as me thinking the demon will crawl back into its hole and disappear forever. Sometimes we see it, other times we don't, but everyone is tormented by something.

I'm tortured by the flattened, urine-infested mattress I attempt to sleep on and plagued by the congealed, spam-like glop they try to pass off as edible.

Jacob sneaks me food. It's one of the thousands of reasons I'm thankful for him. He visited today and brought Jello packs, granola bars, beef jerky and horrible news.

"I woke up," he explained. "And something was looking at me. It was the middle of the night, so I didn't see it real clear, but it looked like your demon."

My heart dove from a building-top and quickly met with the ground. "That's not funny, Jacob."

"I'm not joking. It was in the bed with me. When it saw I was awake, it limped into the corner and disappeared. I woke up Mary and Max. They're at her sister's. Thank God, they're all right."

My head was in my hands. Every time reality seems within my grasp, it slides away as though on ice. How ludicrous, I thought, Jacob has come to a man in a mental hospital for advice. I asked, "How do you know they're okay?"

4 CONFINEMENT

Thorazine changed the definition of weird. I'd been on Paxil and Ativan, but now life was a drooling stupor played at half-speed.

I was sure Father Time was in the geriatric ward of a cosmic hospital taking naps and wheeling slowly down the halls. My family showed no signs of returning, while my uncle in his dragon suit gnawed and clawed chunks out of the door leading to my consciousness.

The demon drew closer and condemned me further with each visit. I smelled it coming. It reeked like Jake's rotting friends.

One night, in the muddled dark of my room and head, I heard it dragging its dead leg. My prickly skin tried to leap from my bones. Waves of darkness washed over me.

A shrill, demonic voice rose from nothingness, and a spirit world opened within me.

My throat cracked the word *God*. Suddenly, I was a devout believer in whatever it took, whatever would ward off hell. I clung to ideas without clarification and listened to the demon speak.

* * *

The next day in group therapy, I was asked how I felt. I'm depressed, of course. Life produces only brief tastes of what brave people dare to dream.

We live scavenging for crumbs from the desserts we craved as children. The promise is cake around the next bend, with a house full of friends yelling surprise.

Such hope is the first step toward God. In our mind's eye we collect ingredients for the festive meal we desire.

Walt Disney said, "If we can dream it, we can do it." In his case, I guess he was right. Now he's lying under Cinderella's castle in a Cryo-tube.

What if you're afraid to open your eyes to a reality you know is true? Suddenly, I knew what I had to do to get my family back.

* * *

The lake soaked in warmth from the sun. A gaggle of geese landed, and ripples raced for land.

Rhonda and I walked.

I squinted. "It's bright."

Rhonda nodded. "You're faster today."

"I stopped the meds."

"You look better."

"That's surprising. . . . My demon talked to me last night."

"What did it say?"

"It's been with me since I was a child. It knows where my wife and daughter are."

"Really? And where are they?"

"Under the floor."

Rhonda looked as if she wanted to walk ahead and leave this lunatic behind. "Under the floor?"

"Well, I don't think they're really under the floor. I think they're in the damn hole he comes out of."

Rhonda looked concerned. "Brendan, you don't really believe that, do you?"

"I didn't tell you. When Jacob visited, he told me he saw the demon."

"What do you mean?"

"He woke up in the middle of the night, and the demon was in bed with him. He sent his wife and son to go live with her sister. Jacob said he believes me. He said either he's as crazy as I am, or I'm not crazy."

"Brendan—"

"I think the demon's stealing people's memories, stealing people's families."

"You know, taking those meds may not be a bad idea."

"You don't believe me?"

"Think about what you're saying. I mean I see shit, but I have a pretty good idea of what's real and what isn't. Trust me, the demon's not real."

Geese swam and honked, long necks craned to prune feathers. A breeze rustled the oaks' leaves. We breathed in lake air.

"Let me prove it to you," I said.

"How?"

"Come to my room tonight. It comes nearly every night now."

Rhonda bit the side of her lip. "I don't know. What if they catch me?"

"What are they going to do?"

"I don't know. Keep us from seeing each other for starters." Rhonda looked past the lake. "I don't know if I could take that. You're my only friend in here. You have to

25

promise, if I don't see anything you'll believe nothing's there, no matter what *you* see."

I agreed.

* * *

The staff patrolled the corridors like military guards. Keys clinked in dim light. Doors slammed, the squeal of their heavy, metal hinges ended in abrupt thunder.

Getting Rhonda in proved to be much harder than getting in Rhonda. She must have thought my words were an elaborate scheme to get her into bed because she was on me at once, sliding the soft contours of her body against mine. She reached behind her back, freed her breasts and tossed her bra to the floor.

I put up a marginal fight for the sake of decency, but months of being alone crushed my resolve. Rhonda bounced and grunted. Pleasure built and escaped my body in a moment of surprising freedom.

The demon appeared, ripped and tore. It lashed, grabbed and pulled Rhonda off me and onto the linoleum. She looked up with pleading eyes. The devil dove atop her with knife-like nails. Rhonda cried. Her lifeblood pulsed dark-red onto the floor and walls.

Helpless, I fled consciousness and reality. Screaming, common to the nights here, sounded from down the hall.

All that remained was a smeared trail leading to where the portal in the floor had been.

I'd simply watched, a coward. Weight crushed my heart and ribcage, my organs squashed flat.

My room looked like a crime scene that should be roped off, only I was on the wrong side of the do-not-cross line—a piece of evidence.

The only friend I had in this place had been slain and dragged into the demon's hole. They're going to think I did it. They're going to look for the body.

I wept.

The staff searched for Rhonda later that night. They found what only hours earlier had pulsed in her veins. I had sopped up her blood using bed sheets, but a residue remained.

* * *

Justice is disregarded nearly as often as love. We profess both as important, yet easily dismiss them.

I was found guilty. I guess in a way I was, but I doubt I deserved the sentence. I doubt I deserved a place where walks around the lake were exchanged for stinging slaps on the back of the head, and my homey room, for a barren cell.

The demon found me even here. It limped closer, a horribly deformed baboon.

Fear and hatred bubbled. I cried out, "You've taken everything from me. What have you done with my wife and daughter?"

The demon narrowed its lifeless eyes and tilted its head.

My tears fell. "Where are they?"

I sensed it got pleasure from my pain.

The monster collapsed into the hole in the floor with the speed of a sprung gallows. I jumped in after it, and the portal closed behind us.

5 WORLDS OF WAX

The Blessed Virgin stood over me, cradling her son. Next to her was Gandhi dressed in a flowing gold robe. Both shared rigid, emotionless stares. The Beatles posed in the next room down.

I trembled, disoriented and afraid to move. Better to be out and lost than know where you are in hell, I thought. The demon must be here . . . somewhere. Perhaps my wife and daughter too.

I searched from room to room but found only tourists and the immortalized. The portal had led to a wax museum in New Orleans.

Amber light glowed in the chamber of horrors. Mist from a smoke machine swirled around tortured wax dummies. Ghoulish recorded laughs and creaking doors blared from a speaker. I gasped and tiptoed past a hooded, axe-wielding lynch man with sunken, watching eyes.

I escaped through a door marked Employees Only. Behind it drying limbs dangled from ropes. Full-body molds were stacked in every corner. The air smelled like church candles.

"You're not supposed to be back here," said a raspy voice.

I peered in its direction.

An old man with ratty plumes of white hair sat at a workbench lined with body parts and historic clothes.

He looked up from under his magnifying glasses. "Who are you supposed to be?"

"Nobody."

"You look like you escaped from somewhere."

I tried to think up a story. I stood there like the escaped convict I was, waiting for him to call for help.

He only sat there, eyeing me, fiddling with a wax nose on the end of a stick. "What do you want?"

I looked around. Manikin heads lined a workbench, each with its own wig. Containers with paints, glass eyes, and fingernails rested on shelves.

"Did you make all these?" I asked.

He placed the nose and stick on the table and wheeled towards me. "Every one of them."

I realized why he didn't stand. "They're very nice."

His wrinkles contorted as if to say his creations weren't intended to be nice.

"True works of art," I said. "Great detail."

"What do you want?"

"I'm looking for my wife and daughter."

His lips curled. "Are they made of wax?"

"No."

"Then they're not in here. They must be in the museum." He wheeled his chair up a ramp, through the door and into the torture chamber beyond. I tagged behind.

We searched for Jane and Ashley among the frigid gazes of statues. All the while, I wondered how I'd ended up in New Orleans.

"Most of these have Nixon's body," said Charlie. "I molded breasts and put the head of Liz Taylor on that one. Making titties is my favorite part."

He was an old man playing with dolls—looking for something to control. I imagined that when the tourists had left for the day, he wheeled from one unresponsive friend to another talking into their hardened ears, then lamenting when his creations failed to answer.

Charlie lived behind another door intended for employees, in a home filled with Formica.

He invited me in for a beer. We drank through the night.

I found out Charlie was a hero. He was in three campaigns of the Second World War, choosing twice to return to his unit when he could have gone home. We shared our stories, both leaving out terrifying details.

Late into the night, after several attempts to call Jacob had failed, I realized the reason the demon had come here.

A woman as frail as antique porcelain staggered into the living room. Half of Charlie's mouth winced. The other half accepted a bottle. "Good morning, Gypsy." He swallowed.

She looked bewildered. "Where am I?"

"You're home, and you need to go back to sleep." He led her back into the bedroom, turned on the television and reappeared minutes later.

"That's Gypsy," he said. "She's got Alzheimer's, if you know anything about that."

I nodded. "Your wife?"

"Close enough."

* * *

Gradually, I realized that hell did not come for my wife, daughter, Rhonda or poor Mr. Carris as much as it had come for me. The demon picked at the scraps of sanity left on my plate. I knew that running, like so many others had, would only tire my soul.

Past the door, in the darkened bedroom, an infomercial flashed electronic promises—nurture for the hopeless.

"That must be hard," I said.

Charlie guzzled a bottle of Budweiser. "What?"

"Living with someone who barely remembers you."

Charlie's face flushed with sorrow. "Hell, people only remember what they want to remember. They only know what they want to know. It's easier than it used to be."

I nodded.

He wheeled himself toward the flashing darkness in the bedroom. "You can sleep on the couch, if you want."

* * *

I'd never rested so well on a couch. Bananas and oatmeal tasted like a king's breakfast. Gypsy glared at me between spoonfuls.

Charlie sat at the head of the table with a bowl of Cheerios, two pieces of buttered toast and a Pabst Blue Ribbon.

The sounds of the torture chamber sparked to life in the museum. I glanced at the door.

Charlie chomped on toast. "That's on a timer."

Gypsy's head dropped and hung close to her bowl of cornflakes. She cocked her head toward me unnaturally— moving as the insane move. Her eyes were a rapidly blinking night. She slurred. "What did it tell you?" She mumbled, spitting out unintelligible words. Not English and nothing I knew.

I looked at Charlie after Gypsy had slunk back into a stupor. "She does that," he said.

"Do you believe in demons?" I asked.

He laughed. "The doctors have a name for that."

"What if I was to tell you a demon visits Gypsy and causes her to forget things?"

He looked uneasy. "I'd say you were crazy. Are you one of those religious nuts?"

Charlie wheeled closer, a serious look on his craggy face. "Are you crazy?"

"Not that I'm aware."

"What you're saying don't sound too sane."

"Do you believe in God?" I asked.

Charlie thought for a moment. "Yeah."

"If you believe in God is it so hard to believe in the devil?"

Faith didn't come easily for Charlie. Genuine faith comes as easily as the hardest things in life. As difficult as this crippled man's life was, I'd have thought he'd be swimming in faith.

I filled in the details of my story. I told Charlie about my wife and daughter kidnapped by a demon and my search for them. I told him about the people at Spencer Meats forgetting Jack Carris.

Charlie gulped beer and belched. "You expect me to buy that?"

"No. I just want you to consider the possibility something may be causing Gypsy to forget."

The television droned out advertisements from the bedroom.

Charlie looked as if he were thinking. "Do you have any idea how crazy you sound?"

"What do you have to lose?"

After breakfast, Charlie gave me a new set of clothes: a white, rhinestone-studded shirt once worn by the wax figure of Elvis, and an old pair of blue-jeans so large I had to cuff the legs and strap the waist with a worn leather belt.

Sometimes desperation makes the best of friends. I don't think he actually believed the things I said. We were both just happy to have someone else around.

Charlie flopped a phonebook open on his lap, pointed to a listing and held up keys. "I think there's someone you should talk to."

Fortunately, the museum was closed on Mondays. I drove Charlie to a beige store with faded lettering that said *New Horizon Books and Things*.

Inside was a Pagan sanctuary laden with smoky incense and shelves lined with New Age and Wicca books. Behind a rustic counter were towering stacks of wood boxes labeled with the names of various herbs and crystals: Coltsfoot, Dragon's Blood, Mugwart, Danburite.

An obese man with chaotic blond hair appeared in the back of the store wearing an evergreen wool gown. "I'm Larry. May I help you?" He moved better than you'd think through the suffocatingly narrow aisles of his store, dodging a rack of leather-strung amethysts and rotating past hundreds of candles. He made his way toward us, his only customers.

"I hope so," I said. "What do you know about demons?"

"What do you want to know?"

"We're looking for someone to help us with a demon that's causing people to forget things."

Charlie wheeled himself to a table and picked up a small ceramic skull with a candle sticking out of it. "Not sure you remember. I came in here a few years back, after my sister passed away." Charlie winced. "I wanted to contact her."

"You probably talked to Karl," said Larry. "He's moved to Birmingham. I can dig up his number if you'd like."

"Yes, that's right," said Charlie.

"Have you seen the demon?" asked Larry.

"It's horribly deformed," I said, "with beady eyes."

Larry nodded. "Does it speak?"

Charlie stared at me blankly. I wondered if he thought me insane.

"Yes."

"And what did it say?"

I paused and gathered my words. "It said it'd been with me since I was a child. That it knew where my wife and daughter are."

Larry looked concerned. "Where did it say they were?"

"Under the ground," I said.

"Wait here." He ducked into the back and returned carrying a worn, black-leather book with scarlet symbols on its cover. "Addicere," said Larry, leafing through the pages. "Pretty sure you're talking about an Addicere. Have you or anyone in your family ever been involved in sorcery, divination, anything like that?"

I shook my head.

"What about your lineage?"

I shrugged. "I don't know."

"Addicere are often attached to families."

Charlie looked curious and quietly watched from his wheelchair.

"What do you mean 'attached?'" I asked.

Larry thought for a moment. "Like a parasite," he said, closing one of his large hands over the other. If you two are serious about this—"

"We're serious," I said.

"Then go see her." Larry handed me a card.

The card read *Mademoiselle Rane, Astrologist, Genealogical Research.*

"I need to know more about you in order to help," said Larry.

* * *

I made an appointment with the Mademoiselle and drove to see her the next day. Charlie stayed at the museum and labored on Princess Diana's head.

CHRISTOPHER HAWKE

Mademoiselle Rane worked out of her home on Lake Street. There wasn't a lake in sight amongst the urban sprawl.

She answered the door. "You caught me before I had time to change into my work clothes."

Her body was covered with paint-dappled corduroy overalls. Her long brown hair was tied into a cat-toy bun. Paint fumes hammered at my head and lungs. I followed her down a hall and into a room with more charts than an architect's office.

She eyed my rhinestone-studded shirt. "You a singer?"

I shook my head.

She smiled. "I'll take payment up front."

I handed her seven twenty-dollar bills, which she quickly pocketed.

"If Larry's sent you, it probably means you're *not* looking to find out if your family floated over on the Mayflower."

She spent the afternoon consulting books and genealogical programs on her computer. She asked what I knew about my family. I told her what little I knew about my parents, grandparents and uncle. I left with rolled up poster of my fallow family tree.

* * *

I brought the printout to Larry the next day.

He peeled a thick volume from a nearby shelf. "Let's see what you have here."

After several minutes of flipping between my family tree and the book, he pointed to the names *Eleanor and Benjamin Grabbles*. "There may be more, but these two definitely practiced magic." He leaned closer to read the fine cursive scrawl. "It says they were a part of the Snow Moon coven in Virginia."

Larry handed me the book and pointed to the names.

I checked for myself. "What is this?"

"A register of all known practitioners of the dark arts. As you might imagine, these aren't easy names to come by."

"So, what does this mean?"

"It means you're dealing with a family demon."

I searched for my uncle's name and found it beside a stenciled dragon-like demon named Th'uban. The book said the worship and devotion of Th'uban held promise of treasure.

I shared my story with Larry, and he helped me understand the reason behind demons, the way they keep us from the reality that God intends.

* * *

I stopped for a hamburger and fries on my way back to *New Orleans House of Wax.*

Sitting, eating, the world seemed much larger. The way it does when you realize something new. Larry opened a spirit world to me. He'd explained the inner-workings of the universe did not rely entirely on a nature we could see and touch. Like a child finally understanding addition, the rules had changed. He'd told me, "Many spend their lives seeking out only the rules, paying little attention to the answers they find."

6 LARRY'S INCANTATION

Charlie put me to work in the museum. I pushed a broom and captured dirt around celebrities. Their vacant, glassy eyes condemned. I expected Robert Redford and Paul Newman to climb off their stands and grab at me.

Like the ghost of an injured soldier, my demon limped into sight down the hall. It glistened with a greasy, rotten shine, its skin like wet leather. My body trembled, a mouse before a snake.

I ran without thought to Charlie's car and headed to *New Horizon Books and Things*. The closer I got the weaker I felt. I nearly collapsed before reaching the door. Inside, witches and warlocks mingled, robed in white wool and swept by brushstrokes of candlelight. Larry kept me from caving to the floor. He helped me into a room in the back of the store.

Consciousness waned. The world blurred.

I choked out words. "The demon's at the museum."

I saw blood-red symbols covering the ceiling, walls and floor. The candles' flames stole the oxygen from my lungs until the room became a distant glare.

A woman with raven-black hair stood over me. Her dark eyes bulged from skull-deep sockets.

I heard chanting. Strength and life leaked from my body.

I gasped for air.

A frigid hand on my forehead drove me toward the floor. My shirt was ripped open, and blood from a bowl was sprinkled on my chest.

I writhed into a comatose trance.

* * *

I woke lucid, my heart flattened by sadness.

Larry stood over me with a sweaty smile. "You are demon-free, my friend."

My body fought directions. Bitter blood inched to the base of my throat. I coughed and spit. "What happened? Where is everyone?"

Larry wiped his forehead with the sleeve of his robe. "The coven left hours ago."

I looked around. The candles had burned down to stubs. Magic symbols shone gleaming red against the black walls, floor and ceiling. Smoke and incense tainted the air.

"You were possessed," said Larry.

"Possessed? How is that possible?" I gathered my strength and sat up. My chest was covered with smudged symbols painted with blood.

I put my head in my hands. "You don't even know me."

"There are different ways to know someone," said Larry. "I see inside people. If you know someone's heart, you know the person. You were fortunate the coven was meeting when you came by."

Tears fell. "How could I have had the demon in me, if I saw the damn thing in the museum?"

"You didn't see the one in you. You must have seen the Addicere. A lesser demon doesn't have the power to stay if you don't want it to. An Addicere is different."

I reached out my hand. "I feel horrible. I left Charlie and Gypsy alone with that thing."

Larry grabbed hold and helped me to my feet. "I'll go with you."

* * *

Larry drove.

The sun clung to the day with apricot-colored rays. The world seemed less oppressive like a place I'd want to be.

However, the museum was dark and quiet. Queen Elizabeth graced the entrance, a thickset wig atop her head. Her pasty, mask-like face glared as we stepped past.

None of the light switches worked. Emergency flood lamps cast hard shadows. We edged our way through the museum. I pushed on the door to Charlie's living room. It opened with a groan. Beyond the darkness, static flashes from a television filled the bedroom. I felt along the wall and flipped on a switch. It worked.

"I never should have left," I said.

A guttural voice sounded from the bedroom. "Fools."

Gypsy flew from the doorway in the blink of an eye and rammed into Larry, sending him sailing. He rolled helplessly toward the wall.

She breathed heavy, angry breaths and turned to face me. She spat, "You're empty."

I glanced at Larry. His body lay limp.

I was knocked to the floor. My head hit and jarred my mind into nauseousness.

Gypsy stood over me, her fossilized form writhing, her eyes the midnight-black of a demon. Larry shouted something in

Latin. The demon ran to him and delivered great leg-swinging kicks. I moved fast, took the toaster off the table and smashed it into Gypsy's gray hair.

She spun round.

Everything cracked. My senses—a beetle under foot.

* * *

I woke badly beaten. My nerves burned. My mouth bled and tasted of iron. I hung, my hands tied to a crossbeam of the floor above me.

Water dripped and pooled in the gloom. A glint of pale light shone down a nearby staircase. *Was I in the basement of the museum?*

Crap had slid down my bruised leg and bunched up near my sock. The air stank of shit and mildew.

I thought it might have been better to have remained possessed and institutionalized.

I thought about life in ways I never had before. Reality unfolded like origami. Some have miniature folding boxes, others great flying swans, but the experienced man knows they are all only carefully folded paper. My piece felt torn in two. One for the man I thought I was and one for the man I hoped to be. Only a bird without wings lived on.

Those teetering on madness hold keys to doors you know nothing about. You must ask yourself if these rooms are worth visiting—if in the end life would have made more sense having been in them.

Brendan McGovern - Seminar May 9th

7 FACING THE MADNESS

In 1492 Columbus sailed the ocean blue, or so the story goes. The pilgrims that followed were saved that first winter by the indigenous people. What's not written in books is that Indians recognized the eyes of those carrying unclean spirits and discretely plucked them out. Pilgrims were willing to cast a few lunatics to the wild, in order to be fed by the natives and survive starvation.

Pioneers encountering decedents of these savages sometimes faked the crazies in hopes of being left alone. Fear of catching the fever of possession sometimes drove the hunting party away. Other times, the raving white were enslaved, or worse, buried in ant hills. But, that was to come much later.

This too is how we survive, falling with brutal force into the institutionalized despair of daily life.

Demons traveled to the new world hiding behind barrels in the hulls of ships and burrowing deep into the hearts of men. It is nothing you will learn in school. I learned it from Larry.

I too starved and ached and reached out with the remnants of my psyche for something, the way those first pilgrims had done.

My hands were tied to a beam of the floor above my head.

A portly figure descended the stairs. I squirmed and tried to free my hands. The ropes burned my wrists raw. My arms were too weak to pull myself up. I hung. The figure walked closer.

Larry cut the ropes, and I collapsed into his meaty arms.

* * *

Upstairs lay in hazy ruin. Water spilled over the edge of the kitchen sink and swamped the strewn-about furniture. The smoky room smelled like a barbeque gone bad.

Larry turned off the faucet. "It tried to start a fire."

"Where is she?"

He pointed to the corner of the room. Gypsy lay under a lamp-stand, pillows and a smoldering, overturned couch. Larry flipped the couch and sat down. "I hope you don't feel as bad as you look."

My body pulsed in pain. "Is she alive?"

"She was when I left her."

"Where's Charlie?"

Larry shrugged. "It's a wonder you can still walk."

I eased onto the couch next to Larry and ran my fingers through my sweat-damp hair. "This is all so crazy."

Larry leaned back and stretched with a laugh. His stomach looked like a prize melon under the white wool of his robe.

Despite my anguish, I found the whole scene comical. Laughter seemed a therapeutic necessity, regardless of the reason.

"It's a good thing you still had the ram's blood on you," said Larry. "I think it prevented her from killing you."

I swallowed my own blood and fought the urge to vomit. My ribs felt as though someone had sawed through them. When I closed my eyes, I saw Jane's perfect face. I saw Ashley playing in the yard under the apple tree. "I need to find my family."

Larry peered at Gypsy's contorted body. "I have an idea."

* * *

We moved Gypsy to her bed and waited for hours, huddled in the closet, watching through slits in the door. Near dawn, the air grew lifeless. The demon rose like a transfigured corpse from a portal in the floor. The hot stench of decay melted the coolness of the air. Its rotten flesh twitched.

I shook in horror.

The demon loomed over Gypsy like a hyena eyeing meal. Then, it turned and limped from the room. It was now or never. I looked to Larry, but it was too dark to see. He opened the closet door. We ran to the demon's hole and jumped in.

* * *

Mystery eclipsed cognition. Our senses were consumed by a trembling drizzle that ran the length of our numb, wet bodies. We strained our eyes and ears, groping against the earth. I called to Larry, but my words fell silent. Murmuring rain ticked the ground around us, until it was an ear-piercing torrent—a barrage of splatter.

A cold wind cut at our skin. A new moon rested in the sky, masked by sinewy clouds. Branches of its light exposed the road before us.

Larry stood and lifted his arms heavenward. His robe clung to his massive form. "This is amazing. One minute we're in the museum and now?"

This new world seemed to spin in a dance.

"Where are we?" I cried. "This is insanity."

"Not insanity." Larry reached down, scooped moist soil into his hands and brought it to his face. "The road to health."

We stood on a road with a clearing on both sides. Moonlight shimmered on the forest beyond like a dance on the sea.

I wiped water from my eyes. "Where do we go?"

Larry looked around, his plump face covered with drops. He pointed. "Looks like light, over that ridge."

* * *

We walked for hours before the glow became distinct flames gleaming in far-off windows. We trudged through the mist into town. The buildings were constructed with wood and stone and the lights were from fires. The structures seemed almost alive, the way they leaned.

Cattle moaned. Fowl rustled and clucked in alleyways. The rain subsided, leaving a chilly, fresh world. Thin clouds veiled the moon.

We studied the door of a tavern and listened to bombastic hoots and hollers inside. We spurred each other on with a glance and entered.

Earthy people, of beastly proportions, crowded the bar, drank from wood mugs and sang fierce fighting songs. Their faces were stained with a thousand days of labor. The tavern smelled of mud and fermented barley.

It dawned on me how far we'd gone.

Their tune slowly died as the group craned their necks to observe us. We weaved our way to an empty corner table and sat down as inconspicuously as possible.

A man the size of a small farmhouse with a bushy black beard planted himself next to us. "You here for the battle?" The stink of fish and drink followed his gravelly words.

Larry nodded. I followed his lead. The crowd murmured.

The man pet his beard and looked at Larry. "Strange clothes. Are you a wizard?"

"Of a kind," mumbled Larry.

"Where have you journeyed from?"

"Farther than you know."

"Boys, we've got ourselves a *wizard* here," sang the man.

A hush filled the tavern. Then the man raised his mug, and everyone cheered, "Hooray!" The crowd resumed their drinking and merriment.

"Welcome to Recuperatio," said the man. "In the morning we head to Pugna. I'm surprised you're not at camp."

"We needed a drink," said Larry.

"But you have no drink." The man swept by the bar, grabbed two pints and smacked them on our table.

We thanked him and joined in a sloshing toast to victory.

These men saw us as strangely dressed mercenaries who'd come to fight alongside their countrymen. Fortunately, they were drunkards, who saw what they wanted to see.

At closing time, we were tossed out with the others and found a fire down the street to warm ourselves. Young men huddled around and gave us looks of suspicion.

The sun ascended and warmed the land.

The earth reeled with tension.

Men on horseback wearing the flowing brown robes of soldiers rode into town waving swords and cords, whipped the boys and called out with thunderous voices. They rounded us up and set us to hiking.

Only the women, children and the aged were left behind, watching from the safety of their cottage homes. Larry and I kept pace in a group between two horses. Beside us, hooves thumped on wet grass. Anyone who failed to march was cut down with a slashing sword.

The countryside was littered with anxious men treading through endless green hills, many looking for a way to escape.

We walked for two steaming days and chilled nights without sleep. My legs gave out the third day, and I collapsed before a terribly green valley.

Wind carried the musk of a thousand soldiers and the morning's smoldering fires. A narrow river wove a wet ribbon though the land. Camp was set in a clearing, with thick forests beyond. Everyone except us had weapons and armor. They setup tents and lit fires with purpose and drive.

Occasionally, we heard death-cries from the forest behind us, as deserters were run through by the very men they had marched with.

Larry seemed to know this place, but I didn't understand how.

* * *

My jaw dropped. I saw Jacob waiting in a food line.

I ran and gave him a hug. "What are you doing here?"

His cheer couldn't hide his grieving eyes. "Same as you, looking for my family."

"I can't believe you're here."

His attention darted from one end of camp to the other and from his feet to the sky. He grimaced trying to keep the tears from falling. "I was hoping I would see you."

Larry strolled up and I introduced my friend.

"Are you from the other world?" asked Jacob.

"Very much so," said Larry.

"Larry knows this place," I said. "He's been here before and can help us."

We took our food and sat under a clump of pines, eating and sharing stories.

Jacob drank beans from a bowl. "You wouldn't believe how many men here are searching for their wives and children. Something more than a war is going on here."

I looked at the thousands of soldiers preparing themselves for something they could never be prepared for. Men sat in groups or by themselves and ate with weapons close at hand— their eyes sweeping the countryside for danger.

"Who are they fighting?" I asked.

"Demons," said Jacob.

"What?"

"That's what they've been saying."

Larry stopped eating and stared at us. "That's right. This is the battle of Tigenmore."

"The battle of what?"

"Tigenmore—a battle between demon and man."

"I don't want to fight," I said. "How do we find our families and get home?"

"Your wives and children are being held prisoner," said Larry. They're being forced to build a temple to Beelzeboul."

"So they're alive?" asked Jacob.

"I can't guarantee anything," said Larry. "I only know legend."

"Where are they?" I asked.

"You have to fight," said Larry.

A golden light flashed and stretched in the sky over the forest, making a horizon of its own. The light rained on a dark army advancing through a seascape of black-hearted violence.

Men ran in hysterical frenzy, yelling, nervously searching for weapons and position, tripping on rocks and roots. Jacob and I cowered behind a horde of soldiers.

I looked again to the sky with its pulsing golden sightline. The whole world was drenched in a rich, yellow hue. A million twisted black forms writhed before us.

"Here is the truth! Go where you will, to Benares or to Mathura; if you do not find your soul, the world is unreal to you."

The Bhagavad-Gita

8 ARMED STRUGGLE

How shallow to presume war exists only within the physical world. Battles are waged for mind and soul, where things far from comprehension are confronted.

My voice matched the timbre of the surrounding chaos. Not a battle cry, but a call to God.

The demonic army approached like a black blizzard, devouring land and air. Monsters clothed in scales wielded fierce swords. Shrieking beasts resembling the corpses of horses forged ahead, plowing through the line of men.

Our archers felled half the beasts. Bolts zipped through the air.

A giant wolf clamped a man with a red beard and Viking-style helmet in its jaws. His body was sliced and mangled and fell into bloody halves. The beasts moved with a swift and deadly rhythm of snarls and pointy teeth. The demons followed, passing us with a clash of bloody steel—their skin and bones sliding within black armor; their eyes, ready voids.

Jacob and I ducked our heads and hid our faces. Little could be done for those leaving the world around us.

Forces converged. Steel met flesh and scale. Teeth and blades drew precious life-blood. We were being overtaken. Each man's sin lay before him like an invitation for destruction. Fear of losing fastened itself to our hearts.

Jacob's eyes met mine in a slow-motion world. We took weapons from the dead—a sword and double-bladed axe. We looked for Larry among the bodies, thwarting strikes from every direction. My sword deflected no less than twenty attempts at my heart. It was our hearts these monsters were after.

General Dougal, of the army of men, watched from high on a hill encompassed by mounted fighters and flag bearers. Red and green embroidered banners draped from poles high above to the ground around the horses.

The enemy bellowed curses. A flash erupted from the golden horizon behind the demons and momentarily blinded us. More men were condemned to death, with the sound of groans, howls and metal clashes. A dimly glowing yellow line remained. Hope burned into our minds.

A beam shot from our camp and filled the air with scarlet waves of fire. The demons covered their crater-ridden faces and squealed like tortured swine.

Larry stood with arms raised. Crimson sparks fled his presence like mini-storms. Every eye was upon him. Shock fell like fiery rain on the horde.

Demons flew after Larry, their mouths screeching and boney arms stretched and wanting. He fought them on all sides. Sparks whirled into blistering tornadoes. Men moved to defend him and gained the upper hand.

After what seemed an eternity, the demons turned and scattered. Men cut stragglers, swiping their blades at darting insect-like legs.

A warm, amber light honored the faces of the fearful, angry and brave—both those drunk on life and those in despair. The land was painted with the colors of a fight—a struggle deep in the psyche of man.

Bodies lay strewn on the field. Trembling hands reached heavenward. Others lay in their own blood.

Larry was unharmed and surrounded by weary soldiers. Jacob and I had barely escaped with our lives.

* * *

Larry's heroics afforded us a meeting with General Dougal. That night the General's tent was lit by enormous candles on curved iron bases. He was a bearded figure in shadow, hunched over a short table with many maps.

Guards stood on either side of the door in sparkling armor.

"You served mankind well today," said Dougal. "What can I do for such fine soldiers?"

Larry stepped from behind us and approached Dougal. "These men are looking for their wives and children."

"We all are," said Dougal. "To fight is sometimes enough to ask for."

I cleared my throat. "Do you know where they are?"

Dougal stepped into the light. His straw-colored beard enhanced his noble face. Grim wrinkles creased his cheeks and forehead. He sent the guards outside and lowered his voice. "If any of you speak of this, your blood will be spilled. Do you understand?" His eyes caught each of ours.

We agreed not to repeat what we heard.

"There is a fortress called Septenary, where human children are slaves and women are raped into birthing more of these monsters," Dougal spat.

My soul crumbled under the weight of his words. Jacob turned white as bleached bones.

"Where is this place?" asked Larry.

"Under the Crown of Vanity, to the east, under that blasphemous light. I warn you, no man has ever left Septenary, whole."

We thanked Dougal and turned to go.

"We need a wizard of your ability," Dougal said to Larry. "We have little gold left, due to years of war, but would pay generously in honor."

Larry bowed.

* * *

Night carried off the day from camp. Fewer fires raged than had the night before. Dying light played on the battlefield over an ocean of corpses. The smell of wood smoke and lifeblood filled our senses.

"This is about balance," said Larry. "Nothing more than foxes and rabbits keeping themselves in check."

"How did you do that magic?" I asked.

"Anything that travels through a dimensional doorway is enchanted," said Larry. "Demons and men are on equal footing in this place. We see them as clearly as they see us. Ultimately, this is about health."

"Seeing our demons clearly is half the battle," said Jacob. "I'm leaving tomorrow to find Mary and Max. Are you coming?"

My hand felt for the scabbard of my sword. "Didn't you hear what Dougal said? No one has ever left Septenary whole. What does that even mean?"

"It means," said Larry, "if you even manage to leave, you'll be missing part of your soul."

"I have nothing to lose," said Jacob. "I don't want to live without my family. Are you two coming?"

Larry folded his arms. "I'm needed here."

I looked at the ground at my feet. Two pebbles lay in a wasteland of dust. I wondered if God saw something greater when he looked at me and Jacob or the whole world for that matter.

"I'm going to find Jane and Ashley," I said.

Larry took hold of our shoulders. "Don't worry. You'll find enchantment in your time."

* * *

With Dougal's blessing, Jacob and I left in the morning, our packs filled with bread, potatoes and blankets. We walked between fields alongside the mile-wide strip of charred ground left by the demons. Blades of grass bent under their own weight and gave way under our feet. We hiked through an evergreen land made canary-yellow by tiny flowers. A stream wound around stout trees with other ivory-white flowers. They smelled like marmalade and made me think of Sunday morning breakfasts with Jane and Ashley. The landscape looked as if colored by a child's hand. The monstrous charred strip of land was a reminder of what awaited us.

By nightfall, my legs stopped without me. They buckled as though I were crippled.

Jacob and I made camp near an ancient forest with trees as wide as narrow houses. I felt like an ant beside such giants. Their tops brushed passing clouds in the tepid breeze.

We sat wearily, facing a fire we'd started with flint and steel. The red and orange flames leapt with an energy I wished I had.

My calves cramped, and I pulled on my toes. "Six more days? This is suicide. What if the demons see our fire?"

Jacob's face was flush with firelight. "You're free to turn around any time."

The fire popped and sap sizzled. Its lashing fingers flicked.

I remembered Ashley's birth. The way she slid into the world, defenseless, and slowly gained independence—a great facade that smothers mankind with supposed freedom.

I remembered hearing voices outside my bedroom window as a child. I knew the others didn't see the night move the way I did. I remembered sleeping next to my wife and waking in recoil to breathing that wasn't hers.

"Do you hear that?" I asked, looking at the dark outline of the forest.

Jacob shook his head and followed my gaze. We watched and wrung the handles of our weapons. Firelight lapped onto a hedge of trees.

Out walked the tallest man I'd ever seen. He was a bright, albino figure wearing a white robe. He moved in the gloom as though he were trying to go unnoticed. Yet, I had no trouble seeing him. His skin glowed phosphorescent, from his smooth, bald head to the feet at the end of his very long legs. He stepped like a timid flamingo, trying to disturb as little as possible.

He stretched out his arms, like a church icon captured in stained-glass. "Do not let your hearts be troubled, and do not be afraid."

I paused, stunned by the sight of him. "Why?" I asked. "Why shouldn't we be afraid?"

"Because, the good Lord is with you." His face was soft and brimmed with love.

"What are you talking about?" asked Jacob. He surveyed the tree line.

"Where's the Lord?" I asked.

"All around you, filling the void in things that have void." His hands fluttered like birds attached to sleeves. "There are a great many things you do not understand."

Jacob looked concerned. "Brendan, are you all right? Who are you talking to?"

The tower of a man lowered his arms. "Time grows short. Enter the womb of the earth."

He turned and trod gaily into the shelter of the trees, moving with swift, agile strides until his glowing skin melded with the patches of moonlight streaming through the forest's canopy.

Jacob punched my arm. "Who the hell are you talking to?"

"What do you mean? Don't tell me you didn't see him."

"Who?"

"The big guy glowing in the dark!"

Jacob shook his head and lowered his axe.

"He said time's short and to enter the womb of the earth."

"What the hell does that mean? That doesn't even make sense."

"Of course it doesn't," I said. "I think he was sent by God."

* * *

The journey was a surreal dream. This world was about knowing the person you'd always wanted to be and setting your foot down to it, remembering the person you'd thought you were as a child and rejoicing in its living, breathing actuality.

The sky was ultramarine and bluer than a royal sapphire. The valley floors were carpeted in silky green. The mountains' snowcapped crests helped us keep perspective.

On the seventh night, I had a nightmare. A faceless demon slunk from the forest and stood beside me as I slept. It paralyzed me with its touch. It turned its head like a curious dog does. I screamed out for Jesus to save me. Jacob shook me awake. I lay awake the remainder of the night, listening to the wind rattle through the trees.

The next day, we fell upon barren and rocky land. We hiked and climbed wearily beneath a charcoal sky.

"What kind of a world is it when you come home and find your family gone?" I asked aloud. "What the hell are we supposed to do, kill ourselves looking for them?"

"If need be," said Jacob, leaning against a fallen tree and sliding his pack to the ground.

I sighed. "This is suicide."

"This is commitment," said Jacob.

"Is this supposed to be our salvation?" I asked. "Our way out."

"I have nothing to lose," said Jacob, "neither do you."

* * *

Someone is pounding on a door within you and hoping for an answer. They want to tell us the secret tale of ourselves. The stories we've never told.

Some African tribes believe if you were to tell someone your entire story the audience would actually become you. From then on, the only life the teller would have would be in and through the listener. Some believe this is the relationship between Jesus and his disciples.

How I wished for my story to be blemish free. How I wished to be a good-natured soul giving back to the world, regardless of how broken I was. In the end, it's those things we are willing to die to change that sculpt our story.

Some people open the floodgates of their minds and hearts so memories burst forth like water through a breached dam. Pieces of our lives can be found among the floating wreckage, and somewhere, the presence of God hovers over the surface of the deep.

Inside, I am treading, biding my time, waiting for the magic I thought I owned as a child. Many seek this enchantment. I sought my wife, daughter and the power to conjure hope.

Rage drove my feet, until my breath was stolen in a gasp, and I stood before Septenary's gate.

9 NIGHT LIFE

Great iron posts pierced the sky, each cast with a demon's symbol: spirals, pitchforks, claws. We looked through the metal slats of the fence. Seven gray pyramids stood mountainous in the distance.

We pushed our way past the gate. The ground was baked red and cracked. The air, stale as a mausoleum. An unnatural light shone from above.

Jacob convulsed in laughter, muttered to himself and pulled at his hair. I held him up by his arm. He howled in crazed fear.

I let him go and walked, head high, across the barren land, expecting something to slaughter us. The hairs on my arms and neck bristled.

Existence lost its pulse, but the pyramids hummed with energy.

Jacob's weeping ceased. I looked back and he was gone. My heart raced. Frantic, I searched among the immense tombs but found only rocky desert.

I wailed at the realization that I was alone once again.

* * *

Imagine the first little girl you fell in love with. She gathered wood on the edge of a distant, dead forest. She was young, but not too young, wearing a blond, braided crown of hair. Her burlap dress was tied with a cloth belt around the waist.

Others emerged from the trees, all of them carrying baskets, all of them the first little girl that someone fell in love with. I could not tell, from so far, that their mothers were flesh, and their fathers black spirits clothed in skin. I found that out later.

The girls walked in single file and held their baskets close. I was mesmerized by the sparkle in their eyes, even from such a distance. Each one looked like an answer to a question I had forgotten I'd asked.

Later, the girls disappeared into the ground like rabbits. I found the hole later—a cave leading from the edge of the forest into the heart of the pyramids.

I squeezed through, a worm in the dark, trying to make as little noise as possible, overwhelmed by the smell of cooking flesh.

Death may be waiting, I thought, but Jane and Ashley would know that I came for them. No matter the outcome, they would know I tried.

I choked on the air and stood when the passage opened. I staggered toward a crimson light that creased the gloom.

Singing as crisp as a robin on a spring day soothed me into forgetting things I wanted to forget.

I moved faster, imagining Jane and Ashley among the chorus of voices. The girls I'd followed were in song and feeding an immense furnace, basting before the sweat-drawing flames.

They were beautiful slaves with soot-blackened faces, bruised, slashed and scarred, hauling cords into the fire.

They didn't see me in the shadows.

I wanted to shout, "I have come to save you all. There is a world outside this place, come with me!"

But, I said nothing.

The youngest opened her eyes wide and shrieked, "Melissa, Amber, there's a man creature." Then the others saw me. Their mouths opened to reveal shards for teeth. The sparkle in their eyes grew black. Terror ran the length of me. They fled from the chamber like a pack of wolves scattering from a rifle blast.

I imagined they'd alert their demonic fathers.

I followed the cave, looking for clues to where captives were held and came upon five lofty doorways chiseled from stone.

Foul-smelling sap dripped from the rock walls down the center passage. Torches sputtered oily light into the cavern and burned acrid air. I burrowed deeper and arrived at a stream splashing with diamond-like shimmer.

Shadows shifted around the bend.

Demons were coming. I heard their snorts over the babble of water.

I stepped quickly and lost sight of my legs in the chilled undercurrent. I followed the stream into a cave with a great swooping ceiling, sloshing along into complete darkness, waist-deep in frigid water, my hands feeling before me.

Hours passed.

A side passage with a wispy, auburn glow opened before me.

Throaty grunts echoed like a legion of discontent pigs. I slouched down into the water and peered around the corner. Shadows danced like spirits on the wall. Thousands of demons squatted and ripped into platters of meat set on the ground before them. Their insect-like arms flailed over their heads like giant locusts. They stripped every bone and emptied every chalice tossing them aside in frenzy.

My eyes and nose skimmed the water's surface.

A demon scuttled to the stream. I sank beneath and watched him bend and scoop water to drink. I stayed as still as I could with the current pulling like a thousand greedy hands. A blow struck my back and forced air from my lungs. I reached behind me and felt cold, fleshy fingers. I let go and a severed arm swept to the surface. The demon watched it sail away, then, rejoined the others.

I gulped air.

Eventually, the demons had their fill and left. Servant girls arrived and scavenged for leftovers. They pinched morsels from bones and swallowed them.

Cool water gushed. I listened to a subtle, desperate voice calling for me to put my head under, breath and be free—the way fish are free. It was the voice man listens to without realizing—murmurs from the darkness of his own mind.

I slid past the room as soon as the coast looked clear, searching for footing on smooth and sharp river rocks, traveling deeper into the cave.

Soon the roar of falling water deafened and a cascading gold sheen bewitched me. A billion drops fell from the ceiling of the cave, where it was too dark to see.

On the other side of the falls, torches blazed over unfathomable riches: gold coins, emeralds, sapphires.

I collapsed onto a bed of treasure, stunned by the splendor, and rested. My eyes nearly closed, before they shot open at the sight of bones. I'd been so enthralled by the riches I hadn't noticed the skeletal remains. All around me, the dead relaxed for all of eternity. I was next in line to fall asleep as they had.

Contentment is a trap, I thought.

I fixated on the bones and kept my eyes from what sparkled. I slipped past and onto a new path. Reality soaked deep and penetrated my soul. I was lost and had no idea where my family was. Impenetrable darkness surrounded me. All I heard was water dripping from my shirt and slacks to the rocky floor.

I gave in to the urge, lay down and closed my eyes, exhausted. I fell asleep.

I woke dry, stiff and wrecked. I may have slept for hours or years. I waited forever for life to end.

* * *

A glowing white beetle crawled along the floor. Another clung to a wall farther away. Though they were only bright specks, they looked to me like cities at night.

I searched the blackness, two others crawled near me.

I picked myself up and stumbled through the lightless caverns—an inept mole, feeling my way along, searching for food and water.

The next chamber held the thick stench of semen. Slews of demons mounted women under hanging baskets of fire, gurgling and grunting with unholy pleasure. Some were the same girls I'd seen earlier, their heads tucked between their arms hugging the ground.

The violation seized me like a mouse squeezed until its eyes popped free. I'd felt I'd had a hero's heart, but now I only sobbed silently.

Nausea struck me, and I heaved. A mixture of bile and bread dripped from my chin.

I couldn't hide. A nude woman approached me. Scratches ran the length of her pale, youthful body.

A noise cracked and I blacked out.

Deuteronomy 32:17

"They sacrificed to demons which are not God—gods they had not known, gods that recently appeared, gods your fathers did not fear."

10 UNDERSTANDING TODAY

I woke. My fluids had been drained. Pain shot from my wrists. I hung, bound with rope, attached to a chain that extended into the vagueness above me. I thought of the cow I had seen dying as a child, her helplessness and determination to live. A vat boiled below, steam scalded the lash marks on my stripped body. Human limbs bubbled to the surface.

Fires raged in the room. Men's bodies roasted on spits, turned slowly by battered pregnant women. The stench closed my throat.

My head felt as heavy as a boulder; my soul raped. My spirit was a pool where evil spat and defecated. My mind searched for an answer as to why I was in hell.

I wished I could throw myself into the flames and be finished.

My wrists threatened to snap.

My eyes flicked about the room.

Every hanging or impaled body was as white as purity.

A man hanging nearby looked like Jacob.

* * *

Rapture is as diverse and assorted as torment. Though torment was on its way, redemption was only a mustard seed in my gut.

Something painful beyond words pricked and squirmed, bit and pulled and finally exploded from my stomach. A worm, the size of an index finger, ripped itself from the confines of my body in a bloody, wiggling struggle. It fell next to the vat and squirmed on the floor. Then it happened again, this time from my gut. Five worms in all. I dropped my head and gave up.

The worms twisted out of sight.

A man hanging nearby was lowered into a cauldron by a toad-like demon. The man's scream lingered forever.

Next, the demon showed its yellow-and-black fangs and lowered me inches from the boil. Oil snapped at my feet. I tried to raise my legs, but I was too weak. I pulled, but nothing happened. I surrendered my soul.

Five brilliant angels grew in the corner of the room. Their giant forms brighter than a thousand stars. Cleansing, white radiance washed over human and fiend, fire and kettle.

Hands lifted me from my chains as easily as a father lifting his infant son.

The parasitic stowaways were angels.

* * *

Sometimes belief is the reason for liberation; other times, our own conviction prevents our escape. It depends on whether or not you believe God is listening, if you can cling to hope in the gravest of times. Hope is a precious life force within us.

I desperately wanted to free my wife and daughter. Yet, I knew that I, myself, needed to be saved.

* * *

The buzzer sounded, as it does every morning in Saint Thomas's Sanitarium. The florescent lamp snapped on over my head. Feelings and images rushed past me. The door locks clicked open all down the hall.

My name is Brendan McGovern, and I am incomplete.

I am free to stagger into the future, and I have resolved to never return to the cauldron that would burn me alive.

My feet met the edge of the lake later that day. Clouds gently reflected in its waters. God visits in the glimmering, distorted surface.

I was there, too, soft in the waters, a pudgy, wrinkled reflection.

We spend our lives sculpting our self-image. Some imagine themselves tremendous, exotic vases; others, the spitting cups for workmen. Imagination and determination are our guides.

I scanned the water for God and listened for His voice on the breeze—hungry for a closer look. Perhaps, a look so close that I would find myself in waters too deep to stand.

I stayed on shore.

The morning was brisk. A crosswind skimmed the water. Rhonda strolled up. I was overjoyed she was alive.

My perception is like a vast buffet. I take bits and pieces, unable to consume it all. Sometimes I have eaten all I can, and I am nauseated enough to regurgitate what I once knew as fact into the faces of those I once loved.

I sat by the lake and remembered the way goodness was not as good as you might imagine, and evil was a lot like we are, living for ourselves.

I thought about angels and demons—the spiritual parasites alive within us. I thought about the rooms down the hall, where people beat their heads against walls until the voices in them quieted.

I thought about Jacob, who had stopped visiting, and Rhonda, who hadn't spoken to me since we slept together. Jane and Ashley seemed like imaginary childhood friends.

I knew the wax figures and battles in my head stood for something else altogether. There meaning went beyond the moment in front of me.

Geese snapped at the grass and honked to each other. Crows clicked and cawed in the surrounding oaks. Leaves on the yard tumbled in the breeze. My mind crumbled under the smashing demolition of memories.

I am alone.

I felt a hand on my shoulder.

"Are you going inside for snacks? It's eleven o'clock."

It was Rhonda. She squinted in the sunlight.

"I guess."

Her face was bright. Light glinted off her curls. "Animal crackers and lemonade."

She helped me up, and we walked together.

I looked back at the lake and saw a good spirit. Cookies pulled from an oven by an elderly woman. Grandchildren gathered, breathing the scent of baked dough and chocolate. I saw a couple kissing in a park, their tongues and lips lightly touching.

Beyond that something else was happening, and then, something else altogether—all of it life. I felt the struggle—these people getting through the day, and meeting their needs.

My wife and child are alive and well somewhere, living their lives as they see fit. This was my gift from God, floating on the water. Look for your own gifts among life's wreckage.

11 FULL DISCLOSURE

I write in the kitchen of my cabin. A rental with a potbelly stove and a head-tall stack of firewood. Crystal snowflakes descend in slow-motion outside the window—nothing rare in Fairbanks, Alaska. Sweet music fills my ears from the player on the table.

Rhonda bursts in and smacks a load of logs next to the stove. She's breathing hard and rubbing her hands together. She pecks my cheek with cold, chapped lips and looks over my shoulder to see what I'm writing. "God, it's hot in here. I don't know why I keep getting wood. You just keep shoveling it in."

"I don't know either," I say, "probably just something to do."

"It's boring," she says. "Don't you ever get bored?"

I motioned to my notepad. "How could I?"

Rhonda ruffles my hair. "Are you going to Hubcap Hill today, *like you said you were*? You haven't worked since we left Saint Thomas's."

"You keep reminding me."

"I'm waitressing every night in a goddamned string of railroad cars. The least you could do is check on the job to help pay for this place."

"I'm writing down some ideas."

"And how much do ideas pay?"

"One day."

"One day?"

"I'll head down."

"Good. It wouldn't be so bad if those train cars went somewhere warm, but they're stuck in the ground."

* * *

Hubcap Hill was exactly that, a hill littered with hubcaps and various other junkyard novelties. Automobile relics lay dormant under drifts, waiting to be useful.

The owner, Dave Schroeder, sat behind a desk stacked with ten years' worth of parts catalogs. He was what some called big-boned, and what I called fat. His hair, once blond, was now banana. His once tan skin looked well-done.

Crates were stacked to the ceiling and crammed full of metal and plastic pieces: a basket full of mirrors—rearview and side-view—crankshafts, alternators, headlamps, holding brackets and fan blades.

I spent the afternoon negotiating my wage. I was going to be paid a little or even less than that. I took a tour of the hill. Mr. Schroeder pointed at different mounds of snow and called out names like "Duster" or "Oldsmobile." And I took it all in, trying to remember as much as I could.

* * *

Weeks later, I tunneled. A guy was on his way to get a catalytic converter off a Ford Ranger and I dug in a fury, my hands frozen numb. My overalls were covered by wet dirt—made blacker by the white landscape.

The principle was the same as any work: provide a service for someone who needs a service provided. The work seemed empty, like getting distracted and re-reading the same sentence over and over. Meanwhile, the rest of the page waited, full of knowledge and adventure.

Through the course of a year, Dave Schroeder spent fewer hours checking on things and more time on Lake Tsolmund with a beer in his hand and a line in the water. This presented me with a prime opportunity.

It took months, but I used a crane to stack cars and appliances into a pyramid. I dug underneath with a shovel, making my way past the snow deep into the earth, finding car parts and fragments of a bigger picture.

Rhonda must have thought I was a hard worker because I returned home every night covered in Fairbanks' soil.

Like many important things in life, it happened a little at a time. Looking back, it should have been clear.

* * *

I wore a miner's helmet with a built-in flashlight and a battery pack attached to my waist. I swung the pickax and shoveled debris into buckets, sucking dust and dirt into my lungs.

The tip of the pickax crunched into something. I chipped away at the surrounding dirt and revealed a wood panel. Further exploration exposed a pine casket. I heaved it into the tunnel and broke its top into splinters.

My wife lay inside. Her decayed, motionless frame still clothed in her favorite blue dress. The smell of spoiled flesh reached me.

A steel claw gripped my heart. I'd known where to find Jane and Ashley.

* * *

Some of us are traitors to our dreams. They are buried in the backyard in coffins of their own. Many people pay homage with flowers—each tender petal an acknowledgement of yesterday's possibility.

Eventually, it got back to Rhonda that I was buying scores of bouquets. Yet, she never saw a single one.

I filled my homemade labyrinth with sweet-smelling Lupin, Roses and Yarrow.

12 OFFERING

I grew tired of being a pawn and wanted to be a king. It started when I read about Mother Teresa. She was a success not because of the money she had or because we knew her name, but because of her voice—a voice calling out from poor Calcutta.

I told the gathering that this is the way each of us should be. Eight people who'd been intrigued by my fliers gathered in a rented lecture room at the Holiday Inn.

It was a beige, windowless room, smelling of carpet shampoo, lined with chairs and floral-patterned trim.

The desperate are always drawn by advertisements that promise miracles. The world is chock-full of people who watch late-night infomercials with the phone in their hands.

I was a natural. Though it was a small group and most of the chairs were vacant, the people hung on with expectation. I listened to myself telling soothing anecdotes and stories as though they had been handed down to me by unknowable prophets.

These folks had come to hear a message that contrasted with their everyday lives, and I had plenty to say. Finally, a service I could provide.

I had little idea where my words came from. They flew from my mouth over the audience like confetti from a cannon.

* * *

When I was a child I was told that "Faith without deeds is worthless."

Life is a great big beautiful three-ring circus. There are those on the floor making their lives among the heads of lions and hoops of fire, and those in the stands, complacent and wowed, their mouths stuffed with popcorn.

I know less now than ever about life, but I do know its size. Life is enormous. Much grander than what we've taken for ourselves, so far.

When the show is over and the tent is packed, the elephants, lions and dancing poodles are caged and mounted on trucks to caravan to the next town. The clown's makeup has worn, and his bright, red smile has been washed down a sink. All that is left is another performance, another tent and set of lights. We rest in the knowledge: the show must go on.

Somewhere, behind our stage curtain, a still, small voice asks why we haven't yet taken up juggling. My seminars were like this. Only, instead of flipping shiny, black bowling balls or roaring chainsaws through the air, I juggled concepts.

The world is intrinsically tied together. All things march through time at different intervals but move ahead in one fashion or another.

Though we may never understand it, we are all part of something much larger than ourselves—something anchoring us to the spot we have mentally chosen. We sniff out the rules, through spiritual quests and the sciences. And with every new discovery, we grow more confused.

Our inability to connect what seems illogical to unite and to defy logic in our understanding keeps us from enlightenment. The artists and insane tiptoe around such insights, but lack the compassion to hand-feed these concepts to a blind world.

The interconnectedness of all things is not simply a pet phrase. It is a big "T" truth that the wise spend their lives attempting to grasp.

These and many other things leapt from my mouth into the ears of those listening, and I was glad.

13 A NEW LEAF

"They must be eating each other." Rhonda squashed a spider between her fingers in a paper towel and threw it away. "There aren't any other bugs for them to eat."

"There aren't any other bugs because the spiders are here," I said. "It's kind of like life."

"You've got to stop it."

"What?"

"Everything's about life. Everything's an analogy."

Rhonda sat on an aqua-colored exercise ball in the cabin's living room. She bounced up and down using a wall for balance. It occurred to me that she didn't know how to use the ball. It had come with an instructional DVD, but we didn't have a television.

"I need material," I said.

"I've had enough for a while. I feel like I'm living with Plato or something."

"Plato never got seventy-five bucks a pop for a three-hour seminar."

Rhonda bounced to her feet. "When you start making more than I do you can philosophize all you want."

* * *

Only five months later, the lecture room was nearly full. I said the same things over and over in a different way, and people ate it up like chocolate bars at a fat camp. I'd stand emotionally naked, with as much enlightenment as I could muster, and tell my followers how good life is. I almost believed it myself.

People came to break locks clicked on their minds and hearts during childhood. They'd reached the crest of their life, exhausted and found nothing but an icy mountain top with a clear view of other mountains. Their souls had been locked away, free from harm and growth like abused, malnourished children.

I told the group these things because the truth of the words was so profoundly bright I saw nothing else. People saw as much as they could see. They reclaimed their personhood by helping to fulfill the dreams of their mates. They returned to where they'd buried their lives and dug, unafraid of what they'd find.

I used to have the luxury of such hope, but I now spent the days visiting Jane and Ashley's spirits in the tunnels beneath Hubcap Hill—weeping for yesterday and a nonexistent tomorrow. They became gods—prosthetics for a man born without legs.

* * *

I had some explaining to do at Hubcap Hill.

Dave Schroeder swung open the door to the office and filled the room with cheap aftershave. "What the hell did you do out there?"

I wanted to say it was art. I wanted to say that the cars I used weren't being used for anything anyway. What came out was less meaningful but saved my job. "It's an attraction."

"Looks like a goddamn pyramid of cars."

"Think about it. How much are you really making here? We can charge people to come and see this wonder of the world. You'll easily make twice the money."

Beads of sweat streamed down Dave's red forehead. "I want every one of those cars un-stacked by morning or you won't have a job. Do you understand?"

I nodded.

* * *

This called for evasive action. I called everyone on my seminar registration list, looking for anyone who might be interested in experiencing a landmark on life's roadmap.

I rigged some colored floodlights and charged thirty-dollars a person. By day, the pyramid looked like a modern-art mishap. By night, bathed in the Northern Lights, it looked like hope. It was magnificent—some said life-changing.

A white-bearded man whose breath smelled like cat food asked me what it was called.

I looked at the red-and-blue spotlights blending in the air and remembered the last Fourth of July I celebrated. "It's The Monument to Families," I said.

To me it was a tower of meaning.

People try to discard knowledge of the past. Like these cars, they try to sell off pieces one at a time.

I watched alongside the others, amazed by something different. These people had no idea how singular this monument was. I barely knew myself. Only half of me was aware of the bodies lying in the gloom of its tunnels.

* * *

In the morning, Mr. Schroeder exploded through the door of the office—a gorilla out of a cardboard box. His reddened nostrils flared. Before he could say a word, I handed him an envelope with the words "A Good Idea" written on it.

Inside was one-hundred-and-forty dollars. He thumbed unhappily through the cash, and I explained what I'd done.

Though I wouldn't say things went *well*, I got to keep my monument and job. My pyramid was on its way to gaining a popularity of its own. Some said it was an act of insanity. Others claimed it was a mark of genius. I looked at it as a landmark. Something to remind me of the time I'd lost everything and was free to do anything.

* * *

Rhonda and I had lived on a shoestring for so long I decided to take her to a restaurant. The traits of many couples in my seminars were rubbing off.

I didn't know the music: some eloquent, classical piece. I didn't know what I was eating: some cold, spicy soup with bay leaves. And even though we'd shared a bed for years, I hardly knew my date.

Rhonda jabbed at her asparagus as though trying to catch it. Her cheeks were pink from wine. We were surrounded by people we'd never see again—men wearing black and gray suits, women in well-mannered gowns.

I patted butter on bread. "Do you ever think about your marriage?"

She looked miserable. "Of course I do. John and I were together eight years. That's a long time for someone like me."

"That's a long time for anyone."

"What about—" She stopped herself. "What am I saying? Of course you do."

"I do."

"Why this?" asked Rhonda, gesturing at the table.

"I thought you'd like it. Don't you like it?"

A tall, black man refilled our water glasses.

"It's fine," said Rhonda. "I guess I'm just not used to it. It's a far cry from Saint Thomas's or our microwave dinners."

"Isn't it strange how something can seem so permanent, when it really isn't," I said. "There were years I thought we'd never get out of that place."

Rhonda stabbed an asparagus spear and slurred, "Don't forget, I was in there years before you came along."

"And you'd still be institutionalized if it weren't for me."

Rhonda faked a curtsy and fluttered her hands. "You want me to bow to you like all your people? Ask you how to make my life better?" She jabbed a finger my way. "Do they know you were locked away?"

* * *

I survived because I questioned little. My past simmered like a long-forgotten pot on a stove. The crusty edges of burnt stew were all that was left, and I was hungry. I'd known, somehow, to return to Alaska, but I wondered what had become of Larry, Jacob and the world I'd left behind.

* * *

Later that week, I woke in the woods. The legs of my jeans were torn. Crusty blood painted my naked chest and speckled the forest floor around my bare feet. The world was endless dusk. My eyes darted from one tree to the next as I attempted to get my bearings. I was a panting fox cornered by hunters.

I checked my shivering body for wounds, trying to recall what happened. My few wounds couldn't account for the amount of blood.

Birds exploded in caws and fluttered through the canopy. Then the forest returned to a forced hush. Someone or something watched. I searched for a weapon and found a sharp stick. The tip was stained dark with blood.

Something moved behind the trees. The forest itself seemed a predator, holding still for the pounce.

The smell of soil and pine needles closed in around me.

Disgusted, I wondered if I'd done something horrible and ruined my chance for the future I'd worked so hard for.

The chopping blades of a helicopter approached and hovered overhead. I crawled beneath sap-covered bushes until it flew off and silence regained its strength.

A kitten's meow pierced the quiet. It slowly transformed into a shrill cry for help. I stumbled toward it and discovered a door half-covered with leaves. Dirty fingers stretched through its steel grate.

Someone whispered the word *please* from inside. It sounded like a begging whine from hell.

I unlatched the door. Men and women poured out, tumbling into the dusk-covered world as though newborn pups.

"I can't believe you did that to us," said Dorothy, a slim woman in stretch jeans and a soiled sweater. "You had absolutely no right. What if I were to lock you in there all night?"

No one else spoke. Some looked as though they'd been weeping for hours. Some appeared stunned; others, overjoyed—each one a disciple.

* * *

What could be closer to death than being smothered by pig entrails in absolute darkness, listening to your friends weep, while breathing in the earth you will lie in for eternity?

What could be closer to resurrection than coming out alive?

The right experience motivates change more than any words and lives on within a person like their very own angel, waiting to burrow to the surface when needed.

I remember thinking, as we walked back to civilization, that these people would never be the same. That's what I wanted— to change the world one person at a time. If it took facing our deepest fears, so be it. We all deserved a chance to face the demons that could rob us of life. If we were mangled by their grasp, perhaps we would wake from the slumber we called life. Only survivors deserved salvation.

* * *

Life laid itself before me like the most beautiful of women. We'd danced, and now it was time to retreat into her arms and know what she had to offer.

I'd imagined something grand—a universe for people unsatisfied in their own. Watching the group crawl out of the ground was like watching children being born of the earth. I marveled at their first steps.

We'd all lost ourselves and found something far more significant together. We reached with gaping wounds for a healing we desired so badly, like a blind man picturing the world around him—the lively children skipping rope, green grass, blue sky. It's like that man standing in his vision, rising from the park bench, arms outstretched, taking the first steps into a world he only hopes exists.

* * *

"I have something I want to show you," I said.

The fringes of Rhonda's waitress's uniform splayed beneath a down jacket. Her muscular legs protruded like spandex-covered pillars.

She stopped in the doorway for a moment and crossed her arms. "What?"

I moved to the door. "It's at Hubcap Hill."

"You've got to be kidding. I'm not going out there. It's fifteen degrees and nearly two in the morning."

* * *

Forty minutes later, we stood in front of the pyramid's dark outline and I connected the lights. Frigid air sliced through our coats. Red and blue light shot heavenward illuminating my creation.

Rhonda laughed. "I don't believe you. Is this what you've been working on all this time? You really are crazy."

"It's a monument," I said.

I took Rhonda through the cab of a Toyota pickup at the bottom. There the ground plummeted into a tunnel.

"A cave," she squealed.

She was loving it, as I knew she would.

Dead flowers lined the passage; their aromas replaced the hollow smell of dirt and decay.

In the depths of the dark, Rhonda saw the caskets, and life stopped for her. I could see it. She froze in abject horror. I could tell she didn't understand.

"It's my family," I said, the words spilling into lunacy. "It's a monument to them."

Rhonda spoke as though her words could change the truth. "A joke?" Her eyes looked ready to burst within their sockets. "Right?"

"It's important for you to know what this is," I said, sliding the top of my daughter's coffin onto the ground.

Rhonda bubbled out a scream. She shook uncontrollably.

I moved to console her, and she ran, tearing up the hole.

When I got to the top, she'd vanished. I waited by the car for hours, hoping for her return.

I showed her the skeletons because I didn't want to be alone. I wanted someone to understand.

She left most of her belongings. Even cherished things like her Mickey Mouse wind-up clock and her World War II photos—the ones of the concentration camp survivors and London after the Blitz.

It's the way life is. Those closest to you are in the best position to shoot you at pointblank range. They're the ones waiting at home with poisoned tea—fixed just the way you like.

It must have something to do with evolution, because, in spite of ourselves, we continue to try. We're born without knowing if our efforts will be worth anything, because no one knows what the end really means.

14 DELIBERATION

Jesus was stoned, but no rock hit him. He slipped into the crowd and was found later teaching on a hill somewhere. History tells us that he did nothing wrong, and we sacrificed him anyway.

The day my father died, I assured him he was headed for heaven, though I had a hard time believing in something that floated so aimlessly through the minds of children. The concept seemed fair and unfair in such equal amounts that it appeared to cancel itself out. I'd never met someone so deserving of eternal bliss, yet from the time I was a child I was taught we all deserve hell. I wondered if heaven existed at all.

But I wanted everlasting life to be real for the man who let me lie on his chest on a hammock in the backyard and taught me not to fear thunder. One of the many things my father taught me not to fear.

His breaths were labored and aided by machines. He wore a white hospital gown. I remember thinking, "I can't believe my father's going to die in a gown."

"Are you afraid?" I asked.

"Not at all," he strained. "I'm going to be with the Lord."

I wished I shared his confidence. For him, it was a priceless thing no one could take.

I wished the fear of death was like the fear of a passing storm cloud—something we outgrow with understanding. For men like my dad, I guess it was.

* * *

Electrical currents jumped synapses and searched the neuropathways of my mind. Some days, I recalled a room down a hall; other days, the foot of someone on the floor. The door opened slowly over time, exposing the scene: Jane, dead on the tile, Ashley sleeping serenely under the surface of her bath, one last bubble clinging to her nostril.

I hardly remember driving them to Alaska, though it must have taken a week. I had found the most striking spot to bury them, a hill overlooking the Chena River. I climbed to the top and found a junkyard. I was so upset, I buried them anyway.

Only a fraction of my mind had taken note of where they were. I still didn't know in the ways that mattered—-the answers to life and death my father knew.

* * *

I slipped around a sliding glass door and through the musty curtains into a room at The Deer Park Motel.

Rhonda sat up in bed, speaking only with her coffee-colored eyes.

"I dreamt about you," I said.

She glanced at the phone on the nightstand.

"Go ahead," I said. "I'm not who you think I am. I didn't kill my family."

"They're looking for you. I saw you on the news."

"That's what happens when you call the police and report someone."

"I didn't call," she said, looking afraid for her life.

I took a seat in a chair next to the television.

She looked ready to erupt with anxiety. "Please, just leave."

I had to know which side Rhonda was on. My answer came shortly after leaving. Two sheriffs' cars approached from down the street.

My legs broke into a sprint. I turned down an alley. One car followed and squealed to a stop. Deputies pursued on foot. I heard their shoes beat the ground behind me. They cried for me to freeze. I vaulted a chain-link fence. Officers landed with smacks on the pavement behind me.

A man opened the door to leave an apartment building. I ran in beside him and hurled my legs up flights of stairs. Feet pounded behind me.

I needed a place to hide. I ran down the hall and jiggled handles. One opened—a laundry room.

A washer sprayed and a dryer droned. I jumped into a cloth container and dumped dirty laundry on top of me. The stench of unwashed clothes filled my nose.

Someone opened the door and stepped inside saying, "Maybe he went down the stairs on the other side."

I held my breath, not sure whether to wait or run. I stepped out and dashed down the stairs I'd come up as fast as my legs would take me. I sprinted onto the street and away from the building.

I doubled over behind a dumpster and drew in rancid air, smelling of rotten meat.

They took my car. I made it home by walking.

Two deputies watched the front of my cabin from inside a squad car. I sneaked in a back window.

Someone had rummaged through everything I owned.

* * *

It was said that Sheriff Burt Cobbs of Fairbanks could track a black bear at night. He had an Old West cowboy's demeanor—ready to draw his weapon in a moment.

I'd seen Cobbs in Pete's Diner a few times. He'd sized me up from the space between his Blue Blocker sunglasses and the side of his face, as though I were not a man but a cougar, sipping a bowl of chowder at the counter.

Burt Cobbs was the kind of man who earned your respect in a glance. Not because he wore a badge on his blue-gray uniform and led a number of deputies. Not even because of the rumor that he'd stayed with his cancerous wife and held her hand until her dying day. There was an underlying reason I didn't understood at the time.

One thing I did understand was that by merely being human, amazing people were both amazingly good and evil and that those who rejected this idea the most needed to understand it the most.

* * *

I evaded the police by staying at a motel outside the town of Ester under a different name. Like Jesus returning to life, I emerged after three days to host a seminar.

Burt Cobbs sat front-and-center between two deputies. One also guarded each door.

"You never know when things may end," I pronounced, "or when something unimaginably good may begin. All we need is space, time and the will to live in reality. We should pursue each relationship for the flame it is in this dark world.

"We are the leaders, in our minds. We have escaped from dictators, floated across seas and cooked in the sun to escape from islands of isolation inside ourselves.

"If your inner world is not broken and rebuilt every day, something is lacking!"

People scratched notes in desperation. I'd grown used to seeing their faces.

The room filled with brilliance was clouded by the scoffing minds of law enforcement. Cobbs looked unmoved.

Afterwards, the podium was flooded with questions and deputies. They handcuffed me, read me my rights and led me away.

* * *

"On May 15th, six years ago, my client, Brendan McGovern, came home to find his wife, Jane and six-year-old daughter, Ashley, dead in their Wakefield, Virginia, home. As I will show the court, my client's family died of carbon monoxide poisoning from a malfunctioning heater. . ."

My lawyer pontificated.

I sat with my arms folded over the orange prison clothes I'd been given a month earlier and listened. The jury's eyes burned with judgment. They looked to the judge for a ruling.

Many of my lawyer's words were news to me. Each syllable sawed at my anchor line. I drifted, relying on tides and currents far from my understanding, desperately hoping to find a comfortable shore. My boat rocked in lapping water. Eventually, I bumped against a rocky cliff, a place where climbing is forever a necessity; and rest, sporadic.

I'd taught people with a constant need for understanding about life and themselves. At some point, they'd learned that knowledge was enlightenment and understanding, a savior. However, understanding has never laid itself out on a cross, real or mythical. Knowledge has never revealed itself to us.

In a sense, we all have our own reality and an ever-growing fear of the actuality of ourselves. This is the reality of which we are truly afraid.

We flock to floods, fires and car accidents like rats to the scent of blood, yet flee from the knowledge that hidden away behind each of our facades is a bland and sterile identity.

Every wish is for itself. Every cry is a child pleading for an absent mother. We are plucked from impending doom and suckle the breast of an identity that is not our own—a self deemed human.

As a child, my mother told me not to talk to strangers. I did my best to obey. She hadn't realized that everyone is a stranger to the part of us that makes us who we truly are. The part of us that prays for the rest in ways we cannot comprehend. In a sense, we are our own monsters, lying in wait under our own beds—our own angels and demons.

The lives we lead will judge us. This is as natural as the sun rising and setting, something that happens whether or not we're alive.

People in the courtroom were hopelessly bound by red tape. A court reporter in a dress suit typed ferociously as my lawyer pleaded. The jury looked stone-faced. I hoped contemplative.

I rubbed the finger where my wedding band had been and wished it were on my hand again.

15 JUDGMENT

Within some people are the kind of magnificent guards you'd find in front of Buckingham Palace, those that wear red-crested jackets and afro-eccentric helmets. Tourists pose in front of them. All the while, hidden SWAT-teams lie in wait, ready to attack if defense is needed.

In the distant past, an innocent man and woman came together in Eden. Christ taught us: they said what they meant and meant what they said.

They had nothing to hide. There was no reason to have guards—ornate or otherwise.

They would watch the sunrise and tend the land. Do God's work and watch the sunset in each other's arms.

The Lion laid down with the Lamb, and there was nothing to fear.

Later, people would fear each other. Denial and rage would roam mankind's minds and souls.

Many of us were taught this story when we were young. Later, we believed it a fable, but the principles still apply. After all, it's not its facts, but the truths we learn from a story that make it valid.

My Eve lay rotting, and my snake tickled my ear with pretty words.

The judge and jury pondered my future. I believed in justice as strongly as I clung to fables.

I took the stand and wept at my own words.

I saw glimpses of the future through the stretched fabric of the universe. A world that tomorrow hadn't yet told anyone but me, and a past only I knew.

My heroes and dreams crumbled like sandcastles at the feet of children. The tide swept away the rest.

I felt as though the whole world were asking if I were bad.

The jury had convinced themselves they were good people, though even Hitler and Mussolini believed their actions were right.

Sanity hangs in the balance of our judgment of the framework and boundaries of reality. Someone is overjoyed because of getting a parking space, while a block away, someone is being raped. We live within a constantly changing perception.

Who are we to judge? However, we must, in order to retain some semblance of sanity, to stand on the edge and admire the view without plunging to our death in an effort to fly.

* * *

Flapjacks roasted. I flipped them with a snap of my wrist. They fumbled onto the stovetop.

Every one of them is an actor, especially the sweet, young waitress putting quarters in the jukebox and popping her gum.

Elvis sang *Jailhouse Rock*. I smiled inside.

I'd never worked in a restaurant before, but I made do the week it lasted. The two Mexican men who worked beside me in the kitchen and the four waitresses eventually realized my ineptness.

All in all, it was two-hundred thirty dollars I hadn't had before.

Russell, the owner, was an Iowa farm boy whose body was man-sized by the time he was fourteen. He was now thirty-seven. Ten years earlier, he could have competed in a Strong Man competition, pulled a semi-truck strapped to his back. After college, when his football career didn't pan out, he took over his father's nineteen-fifties-style diner.

José called out waitresses' names one after another and served up plates full of eggs over this and that, and steaks done every which way.

I used to say, "The past we choose doesn't matter. What matters is where you are today." But, then I looked around. The freedom I experienced when giving my seminars had morphed into a wailing desperation.

I guess Russell heard it. He brought me into his office and offered me another job.

"You suck as a cook," he said. "It takes you twice as long to make anything, and when you're done it tastes like shit."

It was true.

José yelled, "Rosemary." Through the door, I saw him fling another sweaty plate onto the pickup counter. Pots clanged. Grease snapped. Plates clanked.

Russell leaned over his paper-strewn desk and spoke in a whisper, "How would you like to make an easy grand?"

"How?"

"Deliver a car to Orlando, Florida. That's all. I'll throw in enough money for gas and a plane ticket back, too."

"What's in the car?" I asked, even though I already knew.

"Just a car."

* * *

I never thought I'd end up like one of *those* people—a person with so much grief in his past that he goes through life on a steam-train, seeing only the track as far as the next bend. The next station was in Orlando. I wondered what tomorrow could bring that was worthy of hope.

16 A RANDOM TUG

Everyone was on a mission, no matter how ordinary. I doubted anyone was simply driving for the sake of being in a car and traveling at high speeds. They were after something, getting somewhere, and it showed. It's the same delicate balance around the Christmas holiday. People on quests to momentarily complete their lives by acquiring a Barbie Dream something or other. There were toys all over the city waiting for these people.

* * *

I had no idea how it got in, and it didn't matter. Something was transforming. A cocoon hung on the underside of the dash. An insignificant wrapper of weaved microscopic patchwork. It was the beginning of something.

I knew that from high above, the land I drove across resembled that cocoon. An entire world wrapped in a celestial quilt, waiting to be awakened, tear out of its present state, stretch its wings and become something profoundly beautiful.

It was hard to imagine such a big picture while passing recreational vehicles headed to touristy destinations, bumper stickers that said, "If this camper's a rockin' don't bother knockin'." These people seemed busy for the sake of being busy.

* * *

I had no idea I was a celebrity. I ate lunch and read a newspaper at a rest stop picnic table somewhere in Kentucky.

There was an article entitled "Pyramid Baffles Police," with a large picture showing the pyramid of stacked cars. My picture was on the side of the page.

I read on: "Man buried family at workplace and constructed a pyramid of cars on top of their graves. June 7th, six years ago, Brendan McGovern returned home to find his wife Jane and five-year-old daughter, Ashley, had died from carbon monoxide poisoning. According to sources, McGovern's spiritual beliefs may have played a role in his driving their remains from their Wakefield, Virginia, home to Fairbanks, Alaska, where he buried them at Hubcap Hill, a local junkyard. McGovern then gained employment at Hubcap Hill and constructed a pyramid of cars on top of his family's graves.

"Brendan called it 'The Monument to Families' according to John Hearthy, a man who had attended several of McGovern's New-Age Seminars.

Others who were interviewed cited the unorthodox teaching methods used by McGovern, such as locking students in underground bunkers without food or water for days. . . ."

I read the article and wondered if anyone's life had actually changed, or if I'd been living an illusion.

Near the end of the article was this: "Despite McGovern's disappearance shortly after his release, some of the group's members have purchased land in order to live out his teachings."

I chewed my ham sandwich, leaned over my paper and wept.

When I returned to the car, I noticed the butterfly had flown off. I imagined it pollinating flowers along Tennessee roads.

* * *

She wore cargo pants and fleece dappled with dried clay. Wheat-colored locks formed a nest-like crown on her head. She pumped gas into her Jeep Cherokee and drove off with a smile. I followed, kicking myself for not saying something. Fortunately, she didn't go far. She parked across the street at a mall. I spotted her later enjoying a coffee in a bookstore. She had a laptop open on the table in front of her.

I took a seat nearby and pointed to a picture on her computer. "Is that a dog playing with a lion?"

"Yes, it is."

"I love animals. Don't you?"

"I do," she said.

"I wonder how they got them to play like that."

"They like each other, I suppose."

I leaned in. "Yeah, but what keeps the lion from killing the dog?"

"You know, that's a good question."

"I suppose someone taught it not to kill," I said.

Her mouth puckered to one side. Her blue eyes flitted about the room. "I guess so." She turned back to type.

"Brendan," I said, extending my hand.

"Crystal."

* * *

In the weeks that followed, we drank coffee, watched movies and examined each other for imperfections.

Attraction has a way of making you feel as though you're a child with new things to discover.

I fell. My spirit danced in endorphins and neurotransmitters. Magnificent voices sounded in the chorus of my soul.

I wondered how real this was, and how long it could last. It felt like stepping off the edge of a building's roof and finding out you really can fly.

* * *

We sat together on her couch. Candlelight caressed the curves of her body and face. A trail of smoke rose into the air from her red burning cigarette.

It didn't take long before her curious spirit gnawed at the past I tried to conceal. "So, why aren't you still married?"

"It's a long story."

She rested her chin on her palm. "I've got time."

My guards armed themselves. "You're prying."

"Don't I have a right to know?"

"You want to know? Fine. My wife died, and so did my daughter. The heater broke and killed them. I came home and found them, dead. I went nuts. I was institutionalized for six years."

She turned and faced the stack of her paintings she'd shown me earlier. Her ribbon-tied hair flowed onto her nightgown and swam among its frills. "I'm sorry, that's horrible." Crystal got to her feet and strolled to a window. She peered out as if she were looking for something within herself. "I feel as though I'm taking a huge risk by being with you."

I wanted to say I was taking a risk too, that everyone takes a chance just getting up in the morning, but I knew she was risking more. "I should leave."

Crystal rearranged the pillows on the sofa and sat back down.

I'd gotten up, packed my bag and stood by the door. Something made me stop.

The candles were snuffed, leaving only the light in the hall. A line of darkness divided the floor. A picture of beauty, even in half-light, Crystal concealed tears with her hands.

I sat beside her. She smelled like tobacco and salt on warm skin.

"Men always wait until they have your heart, and then they leave," she said.

"I don't want to leave. I don't want to give up what we have." Tears blazed a path down my face. "I haven't wept with a woman in a very long time." I took her hand. "All we have is hope. Will you hope with me?"

Crystal peeked in my direction. "I can't imagine you saying anything else that would have mattered."

* * *

Crystal and I didn't know how long we'd be together, but no one ever does. I thought of how Charlie had stayed with Gypsy, even though she had Alzheimer's and had kept a demon of her own. I thought back to the way my wife and I would lie in bed and dream. A part of me asked how this could be different. And it didn't matter, because it was real now, and that's all we have. Love based solely on hope and the present moment.

It's not that we deserve it. God help us if we get what we deserve. Love, joy and happiness belong to us. They are ours to take, just as pain and disappointment are handed to us the day we're born.

"I have Multiple Sclerosis," said Crystal.

Of course you do, I thought.

I hadn't realized until then how alive she'd become for me, or how fast she was dying.

Having the woman I love look me in the eyes and tell me she was dying was exactly what I needed. She helped me make another attempt at pinning life to the mat.

I thought of Sheriff Cobbs, who stayed with his wife as cancer ate her bones. The only man I'd ever met with such courage. I thought of the men and women attending my seminars, trying to rekindle as much love as they could. It seemed to me there was some magic in this, something beyond the animals we were told we were, an incarnation of something we'd wished into existence.

* * *

Crystal planted tulip bulbs in her front yard. I thought back to the digging I had done. "I have to drop off this car off in Orlando—like we talked about."

She stood in the emerald of her yard; spade in hand, her sapphire eyes brightening the sky. "Will you be back?"

"Of course," I said. "If I don't deliver it, Russell's the kind of guy to have me hunted down."

She gave me a hug to last a lifetime and a kiss flavored with dread.

"I promise. I'll return."

17 SOBER CONNECTIONS

Raccoon, squirrel and rabbit remains littered the roadside for miles. The scene reminded me of the slaughter plant. I envisioned the demons' stronghold filled with their writhing forms.

We run our roads and build our buildings and homes, squeezing out animals until they are perceived as problems. We move onto fields where deer have lived for centuries and hold meetings to talk about the deer problem.

The world that society wants us to perceive is far removed from the true world. We drive to the store in a plastic car and buy food covered in plastic, using a plastic card.

The road stretched on, lined with fast food restaurants and gas stations.

I remember wishing on the eve of the new Millennium that the world would turn into a horror movie, with cars stopped in the middle of the road and people in panic. To me, this would be an appropriate jolt to the human psyche. Something to tear through the facade we call reality, draped around us like a suffocating wet cloth.

I don't agree with the actions of the Unabomber or Timothy McVeigh; however, I believe I understand why they were so desperate to shake up the world.

I am anxious to see even a pinprick of light through that screen. For some, this is a passionate, transforming conclusion, but I fear for too few.

The real world reveals itself like surprise gifts on our doorstep, special moments that seem above and beyond the reality of others. These times are full, beautiful and meaningful beyond words, even when wrapped in pain.

* * *

Six weeks after leaving Alaska, I dropped the car off in a warehouse district in Orlando. I called Russell and apologized for being late, got my cash and bought a plane ticket to Alaska.

After I landed, I rented a car and tracked down Burt Cobbs.

He lived in a pine house, painted white and left to curdle at the end of a long country road lined with cedar trees. The remains of his wife's garden sectioned the front yard. A drizzle cleansed the world. Wind blew through the weeds. Chimes chinked natural music over a brown, plastic rabbit and painted stones. A statue of Pan frozen in a mesmerizing dance decorated one side of the garden. A ceramic angel with a solemn, bowed head adorned the opposite side.

I rapped on the door, my mind empty.

I heard the approaching thump of Burt's boots.

He slowly opened the door. "Yes?" One of his hands held the door. The other lightly tapped the leather of his side-holster.

"Sorry to disturb you," I said. "I think we have something in common. I heard you also lost your wife."

His finger stopped tapping, but his hand remained poised. He said nothing.

"I heard you stayed with your wife . . . until she passed on."

His face hardened. "What do you want?"

"Advice. Can I come in?"

He paused, then swung open the door.

The house had been decorated in old-country style, but now just looked old. Trout hung on plaques near elaborate birdhouses above unburned candles nestled in dead, wood wreaths. Everywhere you looked were arts and crafts projects gone wrong. There was a nativity scene made out of egg cartons and pipe cleaners. Sequin-eyed birds with glued feathers peered from various perches.

A fine layer of dust clothed the room. Nothing had moved in some time.

A half-empty bottle of bourbon waited on the kitchen table, though the Sheriff seemed sober enough. It occurred to me that this was Burt's prison. A place he'd detained himself since his wife's demise. The only sound was water dripping like a metronome into a brimming bowl in the sink.

He motioned for me to sit at the kitchen table. "What can I do for you, Mr. McGovern?"

"I want to know how you did it."

"Did what?"

"Stayed with your wife when you knew she was dying."

Burt studied me in disbelief. "That's what you do when you're married. Anyone would have done the same."

"Not everyone." I thought of Rhonda's and Crystal's husbands who'd left because their wives had fallen ill. I wondered if the extent of my love was greater. If I would somehow stumble upon the heroism I had been seeking. I wondered if I had the courage to make my world one worth living in.

I rested my palms on the table. "You're a good man."

Burt's eyes narrowed. "Not as good as you might think."

The silence was shattered by a thud from the basement. Burt and I both jumped. The walls shook with pounding, as though a giant beneath us struggled against shackles.

Burt looked concerned. "You'd better go."

* * *

When you live with your demon, the thought of warring against it is as foreign as suicide. It isn't until later, when time has passed, that you see the disaster it brought.

I knew I would never see my wife and daughter again. I had no reason left to fight for myself. Yet, something told me to destroy all of it I could for Crystal.

* * *

The rain stopped, but the wind burned. I noticed a butterfly lying near a painted stone in the garden. It could have been mine. Its blue-and-gold wings stretched against the dirt.

I carefully picked it up. Fatigued, it jittered to my finger and tried to fly.

Transformation is a force as natural as a thunderstorm. We are all experiments in our own potential and fleeting beauty. The sunlight's brilliant rays broke clouds open and poured out a liquid-blue sky.

Later that afternoon, I drove to the Monument to Families. Dave Schroeder had been busy. Every car had been removed and placed elsewhere in the yard. Jane's and Ashley's graves had been relocated and filled in.

I drove on, hoping to find the commune. I envisioned a lake with cabins and a bonfire with people singing. I imagined Crystal and me relaxing after sex, lying beside ponds that sparkled like trays of diamonds.

Instead, after a day of searching, I found three deserted trailers in a pine forest. In the center were ashes from a fire. If not for directions from a man in town, I wouldn't have known it was the place.

The trailers were unlocked. I was weak with disappointment and fell asleep inside one. I woke later to the sound of people howling.

Two men and a woman were walking into camp. They looked rugged, each wearing fleece, denim and plaid. They were younger than anyone I remembered attending my seminars.

I stepped from the trailer.

They stopped in surprise.

We stared in silence.

I held up my hand. "Hello."

"Hello," replied the young woman.

"Is this by any chance the group following the teachings of Brendan McGovern?" I asked.

The three exchanged glances.

"Yes, it is," said the taller of the two young men. His arrow-straight, russet hair touched his shoulder tops.

"Are you looking to join?" asked the woman.

I walked closer. "Yes, I am."

"That's wonderful. Another convert. I'm Rachael." She turned to the tall one. "This is Matt." Then motioned to the other. "And Daniel."

I noticed her round face. "Are you Eskimo?"

She brushed back raven-black hair. "I'm part Inuit."

"Everybody says she looks full," Matt interjected. "How about you? What's your name?"

I smirked. "Brendan . . . I guess that's what gave me the idea of joining."

They laughed. Matt stepped toward the ring and built a fire.

Rachael walked to a trailer and disappeared inside. She returned with a red cooler filled with franks, buns and beer. "The others will be here in a little while, but we're all hungry."

Daniel impaled a hotdog onto a stick without saying a word.

"Want one?" asked Rachael.

"Yes. Thanks. So tell me, what's this all about?"

An uneasy silence spread.

Rachael searched the ground for a stick. "It's the best thing I've ever done."

"Me too," Matt agreed.

Daniel nodded and checked his frank for burn marks. The aroma made me salivate and reminded me of countless summer barbeques.

* * *

A reluctant night brought calm to the world. A cool feeling sunk in and wrapped around my bones, but the fire warded off the chill. It didn't get dark enough to reveal the stars, but when the conditions were right, the Aurora Borealis streaked across the sky like an unknowable, mystical force. It was no wonder the native Inuits thought the Northern Lights were a passage to the spirit world.

Rachael sat on a log beside the fire and stared into the flames as though they were an intimate part of her. "This night reminds me of when I was ten years old. My mother told me a story about a girl who wandered the woods while her father was off hunting. She was headed home at dusk when she noticed beautiful bands of green light in the sky. She remembered one of her friends had taught her a song and told her, 'If you sing it, people will come out of the lights and give you treasure.'

"She sang the song, and the lights floated to the ground like a strange, green fog. The mist enveloped her, and she became afraid. Little people advanced in the bright haze, only they weren't carrying treasure, they were carrying axes. They severed the little girl's head." Rachael sliced the air with her hand and looked at me with an amused expression. "They left her body there for her father to find."

The two guys snickered.

"What were they?" I asked.

"*Iminaraq*, little demons. My mother used to say that *Iminaraq* were every bit as real as the Northern Lights."

A branch snapped. I shuddered. A shadowy figure moved among the trees. A man hiked into camp. The crimson glow of the fire reached his face. It looked as sharply-sculpted as the Pan statue in Burt Cobb's garden—hard, with inlays of joy. His hair was jagged and black under a stocking cap. Two German Shepherds galloped before him. They greeted us, sniffing for food. A wet, black nose brushed my hand.

The man headed straight for the cooler and rummaged.

Rachael pointed. "That's Darren."

Darren looked up and waved cautiously. Recognition dawned. He closed the lid, strode over and shook my hand. He looked at Rachael, Matt and Daniel. "Do you know who this is? Mr. McGovern, it's an honor."

"Thanks. Good to see you." I pulled my hand free. "Call me Brendan."

Darren smiled. "Where've you been?"

"Jail." There was no use pretending. My story had been tacked to the minds of the nation. "And falling in love." It seemed in my best interest to leave out the part about the drug trafficking.

Daniel finished off another hotdog. "Not in jail, I hope."

I smiled. "No."

"I can't believe it's really you," said the others.

Darren motioned to the threesome. "Did you tell him about us?"

"Some," said Matt.

Rachael nodded in semi-shock.

"Well, this is all because of you." Darren opened his arms wide.

My eyes caught the outline of the trailers beyond the flickering flames and crackle of the campfire. I smiled. The man saw potential. I liked that. I'd never felt so humbly flattered.

Daniel grinned. "I knew it was him. I'd seen his picture on one of the flyers."

The others looked at Daniel in disbelief.

Rachael tried to push him off his log seat. "I can't believe you didn't tell us!"

Jack and Marie Parker crashed through the trees into camp. They looked like the sort of folks you'd find walking the streets of the Magic Kingdom with Mickey Mouse hats and dripping ice creams. I couldn't imagine what attraction this place had for them.

Jack wore a bright blue baseball cap that sported the phrase "Party Animal." Somehow, I doubted it. For a moment I wondered if they were swingers, but shook off the thought.

I found out later that Marie was a talker, but talked mainly to herself. Her conversations started down a road on a clear, summer's day and wound up hopelessly lost in the woods. She'd take you as far as you were willing to go, which for many was the edge of nonsense.

Dorothy arrived with grace and dignity. She was spirit-like, dressed as though waiting for tree elves to spur her into dance. Her Goldilocks mane rested on the shoulders of her sage-colored dress. I noticed her thermal underwear as she drew closer, a skintight sheath under a sundress. Firelight revealed the grooves of age in her pallid complexion.

Victor arrived last. He looked and smelled as though he'd spent all day standing waist deep in fish. From the tip of his filthy skullcap to the soles of his lumberjack boots, he personified the word *burley*. He might have had his mug plastered on boxes of frozen fish sticks had he bathed and visited a barber. But truth be told, he probably hadn't had a haircut or his calico beard trimmed in years.

The German Shepherds welcomed Victor with eager whines, sitting at attention, tails wagging.

Victor pulled two chunks of halibut from a plastic bag and tossed them to the dogs.

We sat in a circle around burning embers, and I visited each person in time. Many had attended my seminars.

Firelight revealed their faces.

The group watched smoke loft skyward.

Somehow, I knew everyone's secret wish was to float with ease to heaven. But they settled for the camp—the truest reality we could manage.

They were rebuilding themselves, scrounging in lost and forgotten places for a meaning so profound that most people missed it on the way to work, at night in their children's rooms and in the nursing homes they wandered. Purpose was already such a dead and rotten thing that it was buried, dismissed and denied completely.

I remembered the judge, jury and the verdict of my innocence. I wondered if I could ever be something as elusive as innocent and waft deservingly into the sky.

The green, rhythmic expanse swirled above our heads and overwhelmed us. I'd been blind for so long that I'd nearly forgotten it existed. I wondered what other amazing things there were to see.

I longed for Crystal's embrace and understanding. I knew I could not rest until I rested with her.

Darren looked like Pan more than ever. He paced around the fire, half his form vivid scarlet, the other half blackened by shadow. The flames gave his words power. "When I was a child, my family took a trip to the Southwest United States. How many of you have heard of Chaco Canyon?"

No one said a word.

"A thousand years ago, the Chaco people thrived with homes and farms and religious institutions, but on that day, we wandered through what was left of their civilization with cameras and knapsacks."

Darren looked at me in passing, speaking from a black and shapeless face. "I learned a couple things on that trip that have stayed with me, memories that fought their way to the top and survived. I wondered if our culture could end. I wondered if those people had lived in harmony the way it was explained in the visitors' center." Firelight revealed his faint smile. "Archeologists discovered the ways the Chaco people built their dwellings based on sun and lunar cycles, denoting a deeper understanding of the earth and therefore, perhaps, life. I imagine they sat around fires not unlike the one here tonight."

"*My* people are like that," said Rachael. "We believe there's an *inua* or soul in everything."

"*We're* your people," said Darren.

Rachael grinned.

* * *

Darren spoke with authority. He was an archeologist who had researched many sites around the world.

My seminars had made a lasting impression. They were the straw breaking the back of his stereotypical life. Instead of simply studying the past, he decided to live out what he'd learned.

I lay in one of the trailers that night, listening to the others sleep and wondering where my teachings sprang from. I opened my mouth, and lessons arrived like verbal instinct— catalysts for change in people's lives.

My words showered hope like a fountain, only, I felt dry inside. I clung to a possible future with a woman I barely knew and carried with me a past I was not yet ready to understand.

We fished in the morning, a couple miles north of camp in a rushing stream, where droplets of water splattered off stones and onto the misty, cool bank. Salmon struggled against the current, their agile bodies allowing only momentary glimpses.

Flies zipped at the end of lines, striking the water with sudden pops.

Darren, Dorothy, Matt and Victor took to the banks of the stream like experienced fishermen, leaving Rachael, Daniel, Jack and Marie looming dangerously close to me. I'd borrowed waders and a pole but had no idea what to do. It seemed out of place for me to ask for help from people who studied what I said as though I were a god.

"It's all a flick of the wrist," said Victor, casting. He stood mid-thigh in the churning current, letting a bit of feather and hook bob past him. The scene—with Victor's grizzly beard, army-green waders and red flannel shirt rolled up to expose his Navy tattoo—epitomized Alaska.

Victor didn't seem the type to wind up with a bunch of spiritually deprived seekers. He looked self-assured and independent. The fact that he led what I would call "a natural life" and continued to seek out meaning beyond the procurement of fish on cold mornings during top-of-the-world sunrises helped me shape my answer.

I never did get it. I was among the camp of watchers, wading or squatting along a muddy shore, waiting for a bite. I spoke big words, but let the others reel in what mattered.

* * *

The blazing evening fire seared the day's catch. We feasted on salmon and potatoes—fish-and-chips cooked the Alaskan way. Never before had I felt popular, let alone godlike, but the group drew in close around me as though I were giving away gold.

Victor stood. "Tonight it's my turn, but I'd be honored—I'm sure we all would—if Mr. McGovern would speak."

The group whooped in agreement.

"Please," I said, "I'd like to hear what you have to say. You all know my teachings, but I haven't heard yours." In truth, I was overwhelmed, without a thought in my head, full on fish and marinating in the tang of pride.

"Well, I don't speak as good as some of you," Victor started, "but I can talk on what I was planning to say before Mr. McGovern showed up."

"Brendan," I said.

"Before Brendan showed up. One of the things I learned was how Jesus fed all those people with a loaf of bread and a fish."

"The multitude," I said.

"The multitude," Victor continued. "He fed the *multitude* with something like seven loaves and two fish. I've just been thinking. That's all we've got right now—what little we can scrape together. But one day, we're going to be able to feed the masses simply with, like Darren says, 'the way we live.'"

Marie lifted her plate and laughed. "I think we're eating pretty good right now."

"Anyway," said Victor, "that's the first part of what I wanted to say. Let's be thinking of ways we can feed others. The world's starving."

"Here, here," cried Dorothy, accentuating her words with a skyward thrust of her fork.

I bit my tongue to hold back a barrage of questions; namely, what are we eating that's worthy of sharing?

I hoped to sample this bread and fish myself. I wondered if it would satisfy the deep hunger Jesus spoke of.

"As many of you know, I was once lost at sea." Victor glanced my way. "We were supposed to be bottom-trawling off Amchitka Pass, but something went wrong. The entire electrical system frizzed out, knocking out our GPS. We were lost without it . . ."

I noticed Rachael caressing the fire with a stare, as though welcoming its heat into her. Her dark, native eyes seemed to be watching everything and nothing all at once.

The others also looked into the live embers. I imagined them trying to connect with the same wisdom the Chaco people had searched for in countless holy fires. Darren had told us they were the predecessors of the Hopi, Navajo and Zuni tribes—that believed spirits lived in everything.

I could almost see fairies skipping on top of the snake-tongue flames—brief moments of clarity overcome by suffocating normalcy. It occurred to me that everything is believable during a glimpse, and it is during these flashes we see things as they truly are—unruly shadows in the corner of our perceptions. The only way to overcome is to act as Rachael did—as we all should—staring into the brightest light we can manage, until any hint of darkness is burned from our vision.

* * *

In the morning, I rode with Darren to his office at the University of Alaska, Fairbanks. Stacks of ring binders holding reports stood like towers in a land of paper around his computer.

"Those are from a job I did in Mexico. Ever hear of the Altomecs?"

I shook my head.

"They built some of the oldest pyramids down there."

"What are you working on now?" I asked.

"I'm finishing up a project on the first Eskimos—their migration from Siberia on a land bridge. The university flew me in to take a look at a site near the Chisana River Basin. One thing led to another . . . I've been here two years."

My eyes drifted from picture to picture lining the walls. Some were topographical maps, others enlarged photos with captions saying things like: Hofstadir, Iceland, survey and Palenque, Mexico.

"What's next?" I asked.

"Camp Aidenn." Darren winked and smiled. "I've spent my life studying other civilizations. It's about time we built our own."

* * *

That night Jack and Marie gave the firelight lecture. Actually, Marie spoke and Jack listened absentmindedly along with the rest of us, trying to interject bits of sense like pieces of dried fruit into a fruitcake.

Any psychologist worth her salt would have recognized Marie's mother-issues within three minutes of shaking her flabby hand. For us, the issues were not subtle, unhealthy innuendo; they were a special broadcast—a message straight from the daughter's mouth.

"Mother always asked me to pick up around the house, but she had *People* and *Family Life* magazines stacked floor-to-ceiling in *her* room."

I was told it was always the same—anecdotes about her mother, the saint, or her mother, the devil. There was no in between and no peace to be had when your mother was your religion.

* * *

The week passed.

I dreamt of bringing Crystal and everyone who'd played a part in my story to this place. It seemed the only way to inject reality into their lives and help them fight. We needed a united front and a place of refuge. No one could challenge their demons alone.

In the morning, I stood beside a rust-pocked, faded-gray Buick my followers had lent me. The group crowded in to say goodbye. I felt like a boy at camp who'd met the friends of a lifetime and now had to wait until next summer to share in more adventures.

I sensed that, more than anything, they wanted to ask why I'd buried my wife and daughter in a junkyard, built a pyramid on top and charged people to look at it.

Darren's German Shepherds chased each other around the spiked needles of pine trees and kicked up dirt.

I looked at the motley bunch—each one peeking at me from within a famished mind. "What are you going to do when I'm gone?" I asked.

"The same thing we did before you got here," said Darren. "Change the world from the inside out. Just like you said."

"Indeed." I loved talking like this. I got to act like Jesus, pretending I had my shit together. "I'll be back. I'm proud of you all."

My first stop was Wakefield, to see Jacob, the person who had abandoned me when I needed him the most.

18 REVISITING A RESCUE

Jacob's wife, Mary, had taken his son to live at her mother's, and then run off for good. Jacob retreated into a dingy bar's solace and lost the will to work. I found him downtown outside a homeless shelter, painted in coats of grime. Shaggy hair hung around his stubble-ridden cheeks.

He caught me in his bloodshot sight and staggered in my direction. "Good to see you, my friend. You here for the food? It's beans and franks." He smelled as though his pockets had been filled with milk weeks earlier. His breath was eighty-proof.

"Actually, I'm here to see how you're doing."

"Fine. Fine. They let you out?"

"I've been out for a while," I said. "Up in Alaska."

"Beautiful," he gurgled. "I've always wanted to see Alaska. Mary and I always said we were going to take one of those cruises." The midmorning sun beat against us, and he squinted away a glint of pain.

"I'd like you to come back with me," I said.

He stared at me with a face that said just add Bloody Mary mix. "I'm not going to any hospital."

"No. There're some people I'd like you to meet."

Jacob motioned toward the shelter. "What about the beans and franks?"

* * *

We drove west through the city, peering out the window at people waiting at bus stops and out on midday jaunts.

Jacob cradled his bandaged left hand.

"What happened?" I asked.

"I cut it a few days ago. Brendan, I'm sorry I stopped visiting. When Mary left, I had nothing. My whole world shattered."

"It's all right."

"I know you think I abandoned you in there. It's just that I was abandoned, too." Red flecks of vein showed in his eyes.

"I know. We need to get you cleaned up."

* * *

For the next several days, Jacob had me stop at convenience stores for tallboy beers.

He snapped one open and took a swig. The scent of malt liquor permeated the air. I noticed a filleted strip of skin where the bandage had been on his hand. "Looks like you're healing."

Jacob examined the red, flaky crease of his wound. "I guess so. Where are we going? I thought you said we were headed to Alaska."

"New Orleans."

Jacob lowered his beer. "I promised myself I would never go back there. Those were some fucked-up people."

"We were some of them."

"I know. That's why I don't want to go back."

"We have to."

"No, I don't. I'm not getting wrapped up in all that shit again. We barely escaped."

"We're going, to save people from themselves."

Jacob shook his head and looked out the window. We zipped by mile markers and wheat-laden fields. "I never should have come."

"No, you should have stayed on the streets, eating beans and franks."

"Don't be acting all high and mighty because you got yourself a car. I remember when you were puking your guts out in the gutter and coming off a high behind a dumpster. You better remember who was there for you. If I hadn't brought you food, you would have starved in that hell hole."

"That's right! Now we've got a chance to help other people. Do you remember what Larry did for us? How he saved us from ourselves? *We* can be the heroes."

Jacob knew I meant it.

The words were cast like a spell, changing the course of Jacob's life.

* * *

Everything is as temporary as a blade of grass—here today and tomorrow thrown into the fire.

Mankind listens to Jesus's teachings as though deaf and watches as though blind.

We hobble forward in the same pathetic state, desperately yearning to see something that might force belief and hear something to convince us of ideas that resist logic.

Every word spoken or sentence written stretches into tomorrow, where we attempt to hope in what we think we know about ourselves. What we say may change someone forever. What we do may tear down or build up entire worlds.

Christians have it right. I can't imagine anything worthwhile without faith or hope. It comes down to what you have faith or hope in.

We may, one day, lie in bed with staggered, monitored breaths and continue to believe in only ourselves. We may have confidence we're going to pull through. But what does more time matter? We'll be dead soon anyway.

How wonderful to walk hand-in-hand with faith and hope until your final breath. Something to afford you comfort until your last seconds on earth.

We borrow others' spirituality until we find our own. Teachings sound like the late-night bark of a dog, an annoying pang without understanding.

Our soul grows by our side like a little brother and tags along everywhere we go. Sometimes we wish he wasn't there at all.

Then, one day, when climbing trees, little brother catches you as you fall and prevents you from breaking your neck. The crux is that deceptive beliefs may have pushed you from the height you'd achieved.

Awakening your spiritual self is like having a second childhood with faulty parents, broken bones and proverbial brussel sprouts.

The human race hopes to enjoy the pleasures afforded by maturity; however, we are orphaned in the cosmos, searching for riches worth our effort.

The earth is an orbiting speck in incomprehensible vastness. The histories of our civilizations, our accomplishments and secrets, great good and evil—these are no more significant than the single twinkle of a star. Perhaps, this is why we try to outshine the heavens with our cities and make theatrical events of our simple lives.

* * *

Jacob shaved and showered. We scavenged through a Goodwill Store in Hopkinsville, Kentucky. Jacob bought a pair of jeans and a mechanic's shirt with an oval patch labeled Joe.

We drove on, the world an insignificant blur.

"Just because we're going back doesn't mean we've got to shoot up," I said.

"I'm staying in the car." Jacob pointed. "Look at those beef cattle. Who'd imagine such a puny looking herd in Kentucky?"

I looked. "What if there was a law saying that people could only slaughter cattle if they were kept in a slaughterhouse and had never seen the outside world? If they saw outside, you'd have to let them go free, because it would be considered unusually cruel to kill something after it saw blue skies. I sometimes feel like one of those cows that's seen the outside, waiting in line for my day to come. I'm just trying to help as many cows see the outside as possible."

"I don't think it matters if you keep your cows inside or not," said Jacob, "unless maybe there's a blizzard. And even then, if you've got good feed, some of that Bermuda grass or hay to slow digestion, I think they'd be all right."

I longed to sit around another fire with people who understood.

Words poured from my mind. My dam's wall had cracked the moment I saw Jane dead on the floor. These thoughts had been in the water. I wondered what would be left once my soul was drained, if I could find replenishment in a new type of family.

* * *

The place had once been irresistible. The girls were young and dripping with sin. Lines on the glass tabletop in the parlor room begged for someone to snort. The girls weren't allowed to touch the stuff until they had turned at least enough tricks to pay for it. Thus spiraled the cycle of their damnation.

We all have these cycles. Most people's just don't include being poked and prodded by stranger's sexual appendages.

Club Seven bore a glamorous facade. Seven golden pyramids shined against a bayou backdrop. Tonight was orgy night, because every night was orgy night, if you knew the right people and paid the price. Jacob and I parked and stood beside the car. The pyramids hummed. The energy of a rhythmic beat coursed through the muggy air.

"Look straight ahead," I said. "Don't get pulled into anything. We want to see if we can get Melissa and Amber out of there."

"What do you think the odds are that a couple of prostitutes are going ride with you to Alaska?"

"It's not about them. It's about knowing we tried."

* * *

Light strobed. Sunsets and thunderstorms unfolded and folded in half-seconds. Only there was nothing so real. Everything was fake. From the breasts you squeeze and the fleshy boxes you put your condoms in, to the men and women looking desperately hard to find something they'd lost years ago and would never regain.

The place looked different. I could almost make out the rotting bones amongst the empty promise of treasure.

We weaved past dancers and into the inner sanctum of what was once our temple. People obliterated their souls all around us. Men and women made of greasy, sprayed hair and silver and gold necklaces, rings and bracelets. We navigated the passages beneath the club. People writhed lost in haphazard sex, in a room at the end of the hall.

"Have you seen Melissa?" I shouted to a brunette with silver eyeliner who was being taken from behind. She pointed towards a door. The sparkles on her face resembled stars—a galaxy around her eyes.

Fits of music pounded and roared. Light flickered instant pleasure and regret. Bills slid from palm to palm.

Melissa and Amber were giving head in one of the side rooms. Their client's knees appeared weak. Melissa motioned for us to take a seat.

The classlessness of the moment thrashed against me.

The men paid up and rolled off the couch to their feet.

Amber wiped her mouth. "I never thought I'd see you fuckers again."

"What are you boys up for tonight?" asked Melissa.

They both stood five-foot-five in pumps and wore the common sadness of lost beauty—a pearl necklace dropped into an outhouse, a runaway girl slapped into crack-whore. It hurt to look.

They both looked as though they were trying out Maybelline's new line of Heroin eyeliners.

"How are you two?" I asked.

"Wonderful," said Amber, sarcastically.

Jacob drooled in anticipation, looking as though he'd lost the fight.

I was beginning to question what'd brought me back here. "Have either of you girls been to Alaska?"

They looked at each other, popped gum and shook their heads. "Can't say as I have."

"How'd you like to go?"

"You know, I don't know about that," said Melissa. "Do you guys want to fuck or what?"

"You know what'd be good?" I asked. "If you two took a trip with us to Alaska."

Amber flicked me in the chest with one cherry-colored fingernail. "We aren't leaving, fella. You guys either get down to business or scat. You're holding up the line." She gestured to the doorway where several men gawked.

"It'll change your lives," I promised. "You can start over."

Melissa flipped open her phone. "Anything more outta you and I call security."

Amber took Jacob to the corner of the room.

"He doesn't have any money," I yelled.

* * *

The girls chose to stay slaves, feed the furnace and consume scraps. The pyramids overflowed with addicts that had lost themselves in much in the same way Jacob and I had. They clung to their animal state as though it were a reward. They never confronted reason. Love swam somewhere deep in these strung-out children's eyes, sunken in the murk of lust and addiction. I saw it past the glare like watching a fish underwater.

Reality shines brighter than day-to-day responsibility, though we meet both on the road to enlightenment. Our psyches are hungry to evolve the way the creator expects.

I'd been re-created so often I was no longer sure who I was or what answers I might have.

Tomorrow I could be a cadaver, and today, who knows?

There are casualties in war. Those who don't make it back to a place of sound hopes and dreams. Some take on their demons alone. They are deceived into fearlessness and trampled by the hooves of their oppressor.

Besides intervention, there is little justice for the thousands-upon-thousands hacked to pieces all around us.

How dare we try to take life to the next level. Instead of merely protecting ourselves or scrounging up our next meal, we have the audacity to hope for something more—a witness for our lives who will survive alongside us.

* * *

Jacob was pissed, but he thanked me in the end. Some people don't want to be saved from anything, not even themselves. Jacob did. That's why he was eventually happy about not getting a loveless lay and a line up his nose.

My heart ached for Melissa and Amber because they choose to stay behind. I wondered what would happen once they were older addicts with nothing worth selling.

I wept for relationships not possible due to denial and dreams locked in the back of people's minds, all of the bits of life that lay dormant until the babblings of televisions and nursing homes sweep them away. It makes me wonder how many of the dreams we had originally have already been forgotten.

19 CHARLIE'S GIFT

Jacob and I parked the Buick in front of a warehouse-style building in an industrial park just outside of New Orleans. The word *Slapjaw* was artistically scrawled in red and white on a sign in front.

The lobby was brushed with stainless-steel everything and neoteric furniture. A pulsing waterfall sizzled in the corner. Long-legged, puffy-lipped models wearing everything from burkas to low-cut jeans with snappy blouses lounged and flipped through magazines. Three men clad in trendy suits chatted into cell phones and thumbed electronic organizers. Everything was deliberate and designer, from the placenta-based earth tones on the model's faces to the blocked-out schedules and business-friendly manner of these movers-and-shakers.

I strolled to the front desk and told the receptionist I needed to speak to Charles Naish.

Her eyes blinked unhappily. "Do you have an appointment?" Her voice was sexy enough to sell dandruff shampoo.

"I don't," I said. "Just tell Charlie that Brendan McGovern's here to see him."

She picked up the phone and sighed. "Are you telling me you two know Charles Naish?"

"That's exactly what I'm saying."

I scanned the lobby. Everyone in it could have been made of wax; it wouldn't have mattered. Their trim faces held both boredom and suspicion. They probably thought we were part of the cleaning crew.

"My apologies," said the receptionist. "Mr. Naish will see you."

We were directed to take the elevator upstairs, where people franticly jostled the workday.

Jacob and I entered a set of double doors and walked into a warehouse-sized office. Wealth filled the air—a mixture of fine wood, leather and pricy cologne. A liquor cabinet, big-screen television and mahogany desk with black leather chairs made up the décor.

Charlie welcomed me with a firm handshake. "Brendan McGovern. You've been quite a spectacle."

I stepped to the side. "This is my friend, Jacob."

"Pleased to meet you," said Charlie.

Jacob wiped his palm on his jeans and shook hands. "Nice to meet you."

"How are things?" I asked. "How's Gypsy?"

"Gypsy passed away a year ago," said Charlie.

"I'm sorry."

"Yeah, well—"

"How 'bout a drink," said Jacob, looking at the well-stocked bar.

"Sure. What'll you boys have?" asked Charlie.

"Nothing for me," I said.

Jacob was already at the bar and pouring something straight up.

I sank into a plush chair that reminded me of Matthew, my psychologist back in Virginia. Behind the solid mahogany doors, keyboards clattered. Someone yelled, "Not like that! Yes, something more . . ."

Charlie's office was like the eye of a deadline hurricane.

He was more receptive than I would have imagined to the ideas I had about changing the world one person at a time.

"Sounds like you're in a cult," he said, reclaiming his seat behind his desk.

"Not a cult," I said. "It's not like we're brainwashing anybody or anything."

Charlie looked worried. "What are you guys doing, camping out there in the middle of Alaska?"

I didn't know how to answer.

"Some of your ideas are interesting," he said.

"What ideas?" I wondered what he'd heard.

Charlie glanced over to the wet bar. Jacob was filling two glasses at a time.

"That's twenty-two-year-old brandy," said Charlie.

Jacob shrugged—the English language suddenly lost on him.

"I tried to keep up with you when you were in court," explained Charlie. "But when you disappeared, I figured I'd just let you go."

"I'm back," I said lightheartedly. "You should fly up and check out what we're doing."

Charlie shot Jacob an accusing glance. "I don't think so. Looks like you're camping out with a bunch of weirdoes."

"I know it may not seem like it to you now," I said, "but I'm offering you a chance to better your life."

Charlie's face tightened. "I'm not going with you."

"You can do anything you want."

"I've got everything I want right here. I've built this company from practically nothing. You know that. You were here for its beginnings. I've got over a hundred people working for me now. I'm not going to abandon them to go live out in the woods. Even for a day."

I frowned.

"Brendan, when you needed work I was there for you, and you were there when I needed a drinking buddy, but you know I've never gone in for this hoopla about your inner world and whatever." Charlie swished his hand through the air as though swatting at a fly.

* * *

I remembered bugs crawling over my naked body. They were in my head. I had been in an isolation chamber for something like twelve days. Shapeless colors and half-images had morphed into obscurity, until they eventually vanished, leaving only harsh, black illusion. I remember sitting in a silent, lightless world and wishing I could hear a voice, even the raspy, dark-edged voice of my demon—anything to direct me into or out of the void. As it was, I remained perfectly balanced, helplessly teetering.

Sometimes, if you don't hear your calling you've got to make things up. I'd imagine there are folks all over the world on meaningful missions they simply dreamt up one day. These people are feeding the poor in Rwanda, building homes in Honduras or beating someone senseless to steal a wallet.

Somewhere in the middle are the rest of us, the prophets and practitioners of the American Dream living off our daily ration of drive and purpose. Every last one of us means well, at least for ourselves. We climb corporate ladders, sit in cubicles watching clocks and touch up oil paintings on the weekends. Those of us still conscious enough are presented with a choice between a wheelbarrow and a gun.

Instead, we reach for our keys and join a dirge and procession on the way to work.

Ladies and Gentleman, this is survival. Possibly even that ugly word *coping*. There's only an ounce of life in it, while an ocean crashes at our feet.

* * *

Charlie seemed dry as a bone. His legs worked fine, though he couldn't walk in the ways that mattered. His own personal war had crippled him inside. He'd been crushed and returned within the fortification of his office walls.

I gave Charlie my most sincere stare. "You're making a difference here, changing people's lives, giving them work, helping them do what they love. I feel I'm doing the same, in my own way. Different people need different things."

Jacob sat quietly near the bar, pouring himself drink after drink.

"When I interview people," Charlie explained, "I always ask them what they really want to be doing in their lives. If they answer something other than what I'm hiring them to do, I don't hire them. I only want employees that feel fulfilled. You saw my team out there. Those people are doing what they were made to do, and it shows."

"It does," I said.

"I've always wanted to sail around the world," shouted Jacob.

Charlie whisked himself across the room and grabbed the bottle of brandy. Jacob continued to pour.

"Don't you think you've had enough?" asked Charlie.

Golden alcohol sloshed and splattered against the glossy, wood bar.

Hands slipped. The crystal bottle fell, tipping in the air, perfectly suspended in a natural equilibrium, before it shattered into a thousand tiny bits. Glass exploded across the floor, sliding like shrapnel from an alcoholic grenade.

Jacob's head wobbled. He brought his hand to his mouth. "I'm terribly sorry."

Charlie closed his eyes for a moment and regained his composure. "That *will* be your last drink."

Jacob nodded and slumped his shoulders.

Charlie navigated through the shards back to his desk and pressed a button. "Martha, we're going to need to get some cleaning people in here."

A voice responded, "Right away, Mr. Naish. Is everyone okay?"

Charlie eyed Jacob, who'd crawled inside himself and was unresponsive, then at me. I sat, patiently mouthing the word "sorry."

The smell of aged liquor wafted through the office.

Charlie reclaimed his seat. "What do you think you're doing up there?"

"Up where?"

"In Alaska. What's it all about? For you."

I thought for a moment, looking at the crystal littering the hardwood floor. "I want to lead people back to the real world. Give them a place they can go where it feels more awkward to lie than to tell the truth. A place where true life is so apparent you don't have to look for it."

Charlie drew a deep breath and squinted. "That's quite a dream, son."

"I want people to experience how everything is interconnected."

"Yeah, well, you start losing me with that one. I'll tell you what. A friend of mine just bought a couple thousand acres up near Fox, Alaska. He was telling me there was an abandoned scout camp on his property. If you'd like, I can ask about its availability. He owes me some favors."

My eyes widened. "That would be great."
That's how Camp Aidenn was born.

20 DISORIENTED SERVICE

Jacob and I found Larry and Dougal where we'd left them, in the heart of the city, saving people. Larry patted a sinewy, black man's shoulder as we walked into the shelter. The man's smile was yellow and brief. He carried a paper sack he'd been given out the Spanish-arched doorway and into the light of afternoon, heel-toeing down the church's stone entry-steps and back onto the street.

Inside, light waned near the elevated ceiling. Chunks of mortar had given way over the years, exposing the building's original brickwork. Several fixtures hung with charred bulbs. I remember them being out before I left many years earlier. No one had a ladder tall enough to reach them or the money to hire someone who did. So, the homeless congregated and received care packages in the semi-dark of the abandoned church.

Larry handed brown paper bags to a line of men whose demons had thrashed them and left them for dead on the streets of the city.

"Look at you two," said Larry with a bellyful laugh. His balloon-like girth jerked beneath his trademark, sweat-stained tee-shirt.

I feared Jacob and I may have changed as little as Larry.

"So how are you two getting along?" Larry asked, snatching us into welcome-back hugs. "You staying away from the dragon?"

"Doing all right," said Jacob.

I nodded. I was glad to be back as only an observer of the battles taking place here.

* * *

We stood in line for lunch.

Jacob smiled. "Beans and franks!" He was handed a plastic bowl.

We scrunched into long picnic tables and spooned in the meal. Encouraging and despairing memories rode on the smells of home-cooking and body-odor. Larry's counseling lived here. This was where I learned new things about life and myself. I remembered men weeping bitterly with snot running down their faces as they claimed new lives.

The homeless moved their hands to their mouths on each side of me. There wasn't one familiar face, though I felt I knew them all. They were soldiers at war with something powerful and grotesque—each pregnant with their own new psyche—something to force the demons into the shadowy corners of their lives.

Most were religious men, I could tell just by looking at them. They managed to meet one of their most basic needs—the need for hope—by trusting that God gave a shit.

* * *

131

It's no secret that we all live within a damning illusion called denial. We are doomed by our own far-reaching imaginations and beliefs that extend into a glorified version of eternity. How are we to live sanely on the earth, with our heads in the clouds, when we are so far from being giants? How are we to claim higher ideals, when God is absent from the conversations in our minds?

There can be no going back, once we've believed in perfection. We are slain by the stories we were taught as children, stories about Santa Claus, the Easter Bunny and a God who cares.

We pass these heirlooms to our children with the same fervor with which they were delivered, never allowing ourselves to doubt their authenticity or value.

I wondered what the view held outside the proverbial slaughterhouse. For a spiritually awakened person, a good God seems the only reasonable answer. If there's no eternal good, then what would be the use of life?

Man lays the tracks of good and evil before the train of his evolution, moving onward into places he barely understands.

* * *

Jacob and I filled plastic bags with powdered milk. We sorted cans and clothes alongside other volunteers. We were amazed by the good being done. Larry spent hours leading men's groups and weaving the threads of their lives back together. Men left these sessions with tear-stained faces. They looked less hard and more at peace, as though they'd been touched by the magic of another world—as we had.

We worked hard that next week, waking each morning to growing lines of despondent people with grimy fingernails and lice-ridden heads.

I kept trying to convince Larry and Dougal to come to Alaska with us, though I was beginning to wonder why. I couldn't imagine them filling a greater need anywhere. There was more reality in this rundown church than anywhere else I'd been.

Larry and Dougal believed God loves us beyond our limited capabilities, and that grace covers us all.

Limitations were a part of every story told at the shelter, and therefore, so was God. People are drawn to a good story for the same reason they're drawn to God: redemption.

* * *

I'd wanted to bring Melissa, Amber, Charlie, Jacob and Crystal into a life they'd never dared imagine.

I called Crystal every night and told her I'd be back soon to take her to a wonderful place. I hadn't yet told her that for now Camp Aidenn existed only in my dreams.

Before I met her, she'd spent a year paralyzed on her left side and had walked with a cane. Steroids had helped her regain the ability to walk.

I prayed that somehow God would cross the boundary into the physical world and work a miracle for Crystal. From the start, our relationship, our very lives, rested in possibility.

* * *

Jacob and I left with a promise from Larry that he would visit someday. We weaved through back roads to the coast before traveling to Tennessee to pick up Crystal. Mulberry trees hung over the road in front of turn-of-the-century, colonial-style homes. We parked and walked along the beach. Windblown sand sprayed our hair. Waves gave up their foamy, sapphire ghosts along the shore. I sat and wrote.

Sediment drifted to the oblique bottom, and we were among it, forlorn, encompassed in a tide and beyond reason. The pull is angular denoting its originality with man. This sea is but a term, a mere concept on the landscape of mankind's retarded consciousness. On dry land you have the ability to run. Here you are a captive audience. Lungs fill with fluid the way they were at the start.

So much of my life has been lost at sea, the cradle of life, and so much of it found—like an amoeba in its size, but with the same potential. People wash up along these beaches, making memories kept somewhere they've forgotten. Their virtue is for them alone to know. These characters are like everyone else, only different.

The more elements mixed, the more like a god you become. Isn't God the creator of all things, like some great meaningless collage? Only we imagine some understandable purpose could exist in all the unique pictures. We are without hope of understanding this all by ourselves. The creator, too, may be without knowledge of exactly what this work of art of a universe is. So we pour ourselves into it, the way he may pour himself into his work. We hope for the best of outcomes, because it has been given to us to believe such things, but how elusive is truth in a collage such as this? Every picture is unique and unimportant without the whole, and yet the whole is beyond understanding.

* * *

Jacob stood with his feet in the water throwing shells as far as he could. They skipped toward the horizon—a single line separating aquamarine from the powder-blue sky.

It reminded me of a story my father told about two men who met each other on the beach. Both were amazed by the thousands of starfish that had been washed onto shore by a storm. One threw starfish into the water, and the other asked what he was doing.

"Saving starfish," replied the man, as he whipped another over his shoulder and out to sea.

The other man laughed. "You're kidding. There's got to be hundreds of thousands. What does it matter?"

The man picked up another starfish, held it up and said, "It matters to this one." Then he threw it into the water.

I heard this story as a boy, but didn't know what it meant. Now I wondered what I could do in a world where everyone wanted to be saved, but no one knew how.

Jacob called from shoreline, "We should buy a sailboat."

"And why's that?"

"Because there's nothing better than being able to go anywhere you want, whenever you want."

"We can do that now."

Jacob chucked another shell. "Yeah, but it's not the same."

I agreed. "So what's your plan?"

"What do you mean?"

"I mean how do you plan on getting a boat?"

Jacob looked at the waves slapping against his legs. "I hadn't really thought of it. I just thought it'd be nice."

"Nice doesn't make dreams reality," I said.

"You don't have to be a dick about it."

"Well, you can get a job and start saving for your boat. I've had enough empty dreams to last a lifetime."

Suddenly, the beach seemed less peaceful. The surf crashed harder dragging away the shore. We walked to the car, shook the sand off our feet and set out for Sweetwater, Tennessee, without saying a word.

"It's funny," I said, later in the car, "the whole time we were at the shelter you and I never fought. It never even occurred to us."

Jacob was huddled in the passenger's seat. "Because I kept my mouth shut. So long as I've known you you've been like this."

"Like what?"

"I share my thoughts and dreams, and you condemn me for it. Like what I'm doing is never good enough for you."

"We were in a homeless shelter! It *wasn't* good enough."

"Remember the hotdog stand I wanted to run?" asked Jacob.

"You were always strung out on coke . . . it's not that I didn't think you could do it."

"All I know is that's why you've got all those people following you. Your shit doesn't stink."

"I just want what's best for you."

"And what makes you think you know what's best for everyone? My God, Brendan, you've spent the last seven years in a mental hospital."

"I'm starting something big," I said. "It's not a hotdog stand. It's changing people's lives."

"There you go *again*, always better than everyone else."

"Not better, Jacob. But, I stuck it out with Larry's counseling, until *he* said I was ready to leave. And I didn't leave my friend in a fucking loony bin by himself!"

Jacob slammed his fist on the door. "Pull over."

I turned and looked out the window. Half a dragonfly stuck to the side-mirror fluttered in the wind.

"Pull the car over," repeated Jacob.

21 LOVE ALONE

There's little worse than being stuck in a car and fighting with a drunk—especially when he's right.

We were days from Tennessee when I couldn't take the silence any longer. I attempted my tried-and-true method of finishing arguments and nullifying hard feelings.

"You're right," I said. "I know you're right. I have a lot to learn about caring about other people."

Jacob stared at the road ahead and said nothing.

"Why do you think I drove all that way, Jacob? If I didn't care about you, I wouldn't have."

* * *

Relationships are quests, complete with ravenous monsters and piles of treasure. It is unlikely that one would willingly partake in such an adventure, but for the incalculable value of being known by another.

* * *

Jacob and I got a room at a motel on the outskirts of Dalton, Georgia. Night fell and smothered our energy. The vacancy sign hummed—a base-tone for the crickets. Scarlet neon cast a glow into a parking lot filled with travel-weary trucks and cars.

Jacob left to drink up what little money he had left at a bar down the street. I took a handful of little, green muscle relaxants I found in Jacob's bag, and sprawled on my bed, delirious with the idea that I might get married again. I couldn't wait to see Crystal.

The putrid smell of sewage swept through the air. I sensed I was no longer alone, though I didn't want to believe it. The bathroom door was open. Something clanked in the tub. I walked as quietly as I could and peered around the corner. A dark figure stood behind the shower curtain wheezing shallow breaths.

I wanted to kill it and send it back to hell where it belonged. I crept to my bag and grabbed my hunting knife. I stabbed the blade though the plastic curtain and into the monster. I swung quickly, striking over and over again. The tub and curtain splattered dark red. The demon lay contorted in the bottom of the bathtub covered with plastic and moaning.

I wrapped it up and laid the corpse in the trunk of the Buick. I washed the remaining blood out of the tub and off my clothes and hands, then cleared the room of Jacob's and my stuff, throwing it into the back seat.

I looked for Jacob at the bar. They told me he'd left hours earlier. I drove the streets and checked other local hangouts. Sickness filled my stomach. Jacob had gone missing—like Jane and Ashley.

I waited in front of the motel watching insects swarm around its neon sign. I imagined the demon's bloody form tearing from its plastic cocoon in the trunk.

* * *

I wondered if Jacob made good on his threat to leave. He had run before. I waited for him until noon the next day, sleeping in the car until the sun beamed straight down and the warm-blooded town of Dalton seemed in full swing. Traffic swished by.

I decided I had no choice but to finish the trip without him. My heart broke, but I felt stronger. I'd struck a blow for the good guys. I'd take the beast to Alaska and show the group we can defeat our demons.

I put the Buick into drive and thought about Charlie and Jacob, Melissa and Amber. I searched for the peace of knowing I'd done everything I could to steer them onto the right course.

* * *

Life is not about what we deserve; it's about the best we can make or find for ourselves. Your pain, humility and anger belong to you. So does your happiness and joy. They're there for the taking and unusable to anyone else.

Life moves us, like an unstoppable tide, pulling us into new things. We have no choice but to tread and look for islands of purpose to swim to before we drown.

I wondered if I could make it to Sweetwater, Tennessee, before dark.

* * *

Crystal was more than a woman. She was an angel filled with grace and love. Things experienced so rarely, it was hard to believe in them at all.

I knocked on Crystal's door.

She answered and gave me a hug I wished could last forever. "I never stopped believing. I knew you would come back for me."

"Of course," I whispered in her ear. "You're my angel."

She smelled as fresh as baby powder and felt softer than down.

It felt right driving north to our new home, a place where we could learn and grow with each other.

Crystal's blond hair danced to the music as wind blew through the car. We listened to Chuck Berry, John Denver and Pat Benatar—Crystal's collection—from a CD player on the front seat.

I kept our cargo a surprise.

* * *

We stopped on the side of the road and vanished beneath a blanket of wild flowers: indigo, canary, velvety maroon, red with streaks of black and amber. Some like eyelashes, others like fat fingers reaching toward the sun. Crystal and I wrestled in the middle of them all, as playful as otters, and as free as any animals on earth.

She grabbed me and pulled me down among the bugs, the dirt and her eager lips. The energy coursing through her was startling, despite her body's failings.

I thought to myself, this is real. I could live in this place. Life doesn't get better. Wind swayed our multi-colored canopy. We matched and counter-matched gentle strokes.

Love suspended around us and in us like a subtle ghost.

We were ready for something only the master of emotions could manage: a change neither of us feared, an appetizer toward a full meal of understanding, words and eyes that spoke tenderly, "I know what you mean. I know how you feel."

Days trickled by overflowing with sweet, hopeful nothings, like a basket filled with gold-wrapped chocolates—the kind you pop into your mouth and the next is always better than the last.

22 ACCIDENTAL RECONCILIATION

I longed for a future with Crystal, spending time in other wildflower fields, working alongside our new family, building a place to belong. Hope became my preoccupation. The best part was this was no longer a lonely hope.

God is good. This possibility is enough, because we need it to be. This is ground-level hope. The spiritual person needs it like the physical person needs bread or water, just as Jesus said.

Crystal and I neared Alaska. We slept in the Buick at a rest stop near Whitehorse, Canada, and I had a dream.

A boy was taking a walk in the woods. Rain tapped the leaves overhead and those on the ground. He noticed the most beautiful pendant made of gold and jewels half covered by leaves. It seemed alive—the way it moved him. He put it on and showed it to everyone he met from then on. As the dream continued, the boy became a young man and the pendant became more than something he wore. It became part of him.

Then, one day, as quickly as he found it, it was gone. He looked for it everywhere, tearing apart all he owned in his search. He presumed it'd been stolen, or fate itself had snatched it up and given it to someone else, because he knew he never deserved something so beautiful.

When the man was much older and was gathered with close friends around a campfire, he noticed the sparkle of the pendant in the center of the flames. Overcome with joy, he reached in and was badly wounded by the blaze.

The man retreated to a nearby stream to cool his hand and ease his pain. When he returned his friends were gone, as was the camp, the fire and the pendant with its splendor. By now, the man realized he was old. He held his tortured hand and sobbed into the night.

The old man awakened in the morning as a young boy. All that had happened was an unreachable, far-off memory, yet he still wore the scars of his mistake.

He walked in the woods later that day and stumbled upon the most beautiful and enticing thing he'd ever seen.

* * *

I woke to a stench in the early morning. The trunk was open. I leapt from the car. Crystal was in the distance along the road with her thumb out.

The realization of what I had done and who I was crushed me like an avalanche of shock and regret, every compressed snowflake a pain of its own.

Jacob stared at me from the trunk in frozen horror, white, stiff and wrapped neatly in plastic. Panic rose; I was a lost child without anyone to find me.

I fought thought and emotion and moved mechanically, cradling the plastic bundle and dropping Jacob's body in a dumpster at the rest area. His body hit the bottom with a hollow clang.

Crystal was hysterical. She stumbled down the highway. I beat down my inner turmoil and pulled the car alongside her.

"Go away," she wept.

"I'm sorry. I should have told you."

"You're such a freak," she sobbed. "Just leave me alone."

I had nothing to say—nothing to offer. A faint question surfaced. Will Crystal be safe with me? I forced the question under, holding its struggling form down until it breathed no more.

I called from the window of the Buick. "Please, Crystal, I love you. Let me explain."

She staggered in long grass. "Stay away."

Three semi-trucks screamed by, then left us in the silent, dim light of morning.

"Please, get in the car. I can explain."

"I'm not getting in with you." She bent over in uncontrollable sobbing.

I got out and approached her. She ran, slipped and fell.

I stood over her and held out my hand. "I don't mean you any harm."

She looked up from the ground. "Who is that?"

I didn't know how to answer—my friend? A homeless man? I had no answer to why a dead man was in my car.

"I think I killed him," I said. "It was an accident."

"An accident? How did he die? There was blood!"

"I'll explain," I said. "Just don't tell me that everything that we dreamt of together is ruined because of this."

"Brendan, this isn't normal. This isn't some relational issue. There's a dead guy in the trunk of your car. How do you expect me to trust you after something like this?"

"I'm sorry." I looked at her, lost in the grassy blades. I remembered us playing beneath the flowers and joined Crystal in flooding the world in tears. "I can't go on without you."

She appeared to be a child suddenly realizing she was surrounded by the dark.

"He wasn't himself," I said. My words hid from the light of logic. "I know that sounds crazy."

"You have no idea." Crystal eyed a quickly approaching, blue station wagon. It passed in a blur, carrying with it her hope of escape.

* * *

It may have been Stockholm Syndrome. It was certainly more out of desperation than love that I was able to coax her into the car. She rode pressed against the passenger door, staring straight ahead, much the same way Jacob had. I'd never felt so far away and close to anyone at the same time.

How can something like love be so unknowable and fleeting?

Denial has always been my friend. She served me when no one else would, bringing me glass after glass of sweet-tasting distortion. I continued to drink, not realizing the only thing I'd hoped in was a blueprint. Plans for the person I thought I could build myself into.

* * *

We pulled into Camp Aidenn outside of Fairbanks. The trailers looked washed-out and beaten by the afternoon sun.

Crystal's hair was frizzed from the wind. Her tired, blue eyes narrowed in response to sudden movements among the trees. "Where is everyone?"

"Mostly in Fairbanks. They work during the day. The Parkers make the drive in from Minto on the weekends."

"Can we go into town?"

"This is all going to change," I said. "Charlie's going to come through with the property. We're going to have an entire camp."

Crystal looked at the trailers, then back at me. "Let's go to town, I'm starved."

"I know you think you know me, but you can't know me," I said. "No one truly knows each other."

"Brendan, I just want to get some lunch. Okay?"

I got back in the Buick and waited for her.

It hadn't occurred to me that I might be possessed, only that I was losing my conscience. Good and evil blurred, yet remained a necessity, as important as hope in something that would last beyond my years.

Possession was nothing more than a disconnect from who I had once dreamed of being—a phenomenon of descent without warning into a monstrous reality.

* * *

Fairbanks was just how I remembered. Louie's Tavern still served good burgers and fries. We sat at the bar and ate to the music of AC/DC and the crack of pool balls.

This was one of the places I had wanted to bring Jacob.

"How long do you think you've got?" asked Crystal, dipping fries into ketchup.

"What do you mean?"

"Well, it's only so long until they catch up with you for killing that guy."

A biker with a Harley jacket and matching black beard sitting nearby glanced our way.

"I don't think we should talk about this right now."

Crystal's leg shook on the barstool. Her words drummed out of her. "I think we ought to go separate ways."

My pleasure melted.

Her blue eyes looked more scared than sad. "Don't worry, I won't tell anyone you killed anybody."

The Harley rider lit a cigarette. Pool balls cracked. People laughed at the end of the bar.

"What about our dream? Our new life?"

Crystal drew in the nicotine-tinted bar air and lowered her voice. "You need to go to the police. They're going to be able to track him back to you. You know that, don't you?"

"I only know I want to be with you. It was an accident. You have to believe me."

"How do you accidentally stab someone to death and wrap their body in a shower curtain?"

The Harley guy, a couple on our other side and the bartender leaned in for a better listen.

"It *was* an accident. He wasn't himself."

Crystal held up her hand. "Well, God help anyone who's not themselves around you. You know getting in that car was one of the hardest things I ever had to do."

"I'm sorry."

"And leaving you is one of the easiest."

"I told you. I thought he was an intruder."

Crystal nodded. "An intruder in your shower."

"I know it doesn't sound believable."

Her leg shook violently. "Damn right it doesn't."

"I took some pills. I wasn't in the right frame of mind."

She rested her head in her hands, her elbows on the bar. "And what about your wife and daughter? They were intruders too?"

"No, of course not."

"Are you a junky?"

"No. I found some pills in Jacob's bag. I thought they'd put me out. I needed to sleep."

"Is that his name?"

I nodded.

"My God. I can't believe you killed your friend. Did you kill your family?"

I looked around. Everyone in the bar was slumped toward us with perked ears. I stared at them until they acted as if they weren't paying attention.

"It's a mistake," I said. "I made a huge mistake. I feel horrible about it."

Crystal shook her head in disbelief. "Forgetting someone's birthday is a mistake, Brendan. Stabbing your friend in the shower and leaving his body at a rest stop is not a fucking mistake!"

I closed my eyes, absorbing the retribution, sure everyone in the bar had heard my name and the place I'd hidden Jacob's remains. "Why don't you just call the police? Call the police and be done with it."

I noticed the bartender was already dialing. He cupped his hand over one ear, as far away from us as the cord would reach, spying in our direction and talking fast.

"My guess is he's already calling," I said. A lump rested in my throat.

Crystal looked. "It's for the best."

* * *

Two squad cars squealed to a stop in front of Louie's. I waited outside, to make things easier. People watched from the tavern's greasy windows. I scanned the voyeurs' faces. Crystal must have stayed at the bar.

Burt Cobbs sat on the hood of his Crown Victoria, one boot resting on the bumper. He looked as though he'd seen enough of me to last a lifetime. He said, "I've seen about enough of you to last a lifetime."

I glanced at my pitiful form in his Blue Blockers: my scraggily hair and hollow, emotionless expression. I would have arrested myself on the spot had I been him.

The deputy went inside to talk to the bartender.

Burt motioned me over. "So what's this I hear about you killing somebody?"

I sighed. "It was an accident."

Burt cuffed me, read me my rights and sat me in the back of his car.

We waited for the deputy to finish inside. He walked out and saw me in the back. Burt lowered his window. "Go ahead and follow in your car."

The deputy nodded.

I told Burt where I'd thrown Jacob's body.

We sped down the highway.

Everything was over. I would spend my life in jail. I wished so badly that I could bring Jacob back to life that I felt nothing at all. My emotional bonfire had been doused.

"This one?" asked Burt.

"I think so. Rest stops all kind of look the same."

We pulled in and drove the circle to the back where the dumpsters were.

We parked. The deputy pulled in behind. Burt walked over and threw open the lid. He reached in, pulled out two black trash bags and leaned down, looking at the handiwork that would plague me the rest of my life.

The deputy had nearly reached the dumpster. Burt turned. "I'll take care of this one, John."

The man stopped, a wave of shock passing over him. He took two more steps.

Burt motioned back to his car. "I mean it. I'll meet you back at the diner."

"Sheriff, if there's a body in there." The deputy glanced my way. "We ought to go by the book."

Burt's face stiffened. "If there were a body, do you think I'd be sending you back to the diner?"

The man thought about this. He turned, got back in his Crown Victoria and slowly drove off.

Burt threw the trash bags back in the dumpster and returned to the car. He took off his sunglasses, rubbed his eyes and faced me. "You want to tell me what happened?"

I told him everything I knew, including the little green pills.

When I finished, he sighed deeply. "You're lucky *I* got called on this one. That ain't no man."

My jaw dropped. I stared in disbelief.

He pulled out onto the highway, and I looked back at the dumpster with Jacob's body in it.

"Where are you taking me?"

"Where do you want to go?"

"Back to the bar."

Burt nodded.

"You mean you believe me?" I asked. "You think what I saw was real?"

Burt squinted at me in the rearview. "Don't ask me how I know. I just do. Things aren't always what they seem."

We parked in front of Louie's.

Burt un-cuffed me and let me out. "Did anyone else see the body?"

"No," I lied.

He offered me his hand. "Don't mention this to anyone."

Inside the bar, I walked under the weight of stares. I was reminded of my seminars, when every eye tracked me. The bartender blinked but didn't move.

Crystal was nowhere to be found.

I ordered a beer. The bartender slid a bottle on the table without saying a word.

"You didn't actually believe all that? Did you?" I asked everyone.

The bartender shrugged.

"Do you know where the woman I was with went?"

The bartender glanced to one wall of the bar. Crystal stumbled from the restroom, her shock eclipsing all others.

She pressed her way to the bar, scooted up on a stool and lit a cigarette. Despite the roar of the guitar from the speakers, the moment seemed silent.

She took a drag before curiosity overcame her. "What happened?"

I must have been an apparition, swimming in her diluted, liquor gaze.

"I don't know," I said honestly.

She poked at me with the cigarette-endowed hand. "This is one fucked up world if they let you go."

"I thought you already knew that."

A smile turned up the corners of her mouth. "You're actually one of the more incredible people I've met." She swayed as though she were on a ship in rough seas.

"I truly love you," I said. "I wouldn't have come back if I didn't, either time. I have your best interest in mind."

Pool balls cracked.

She drew in smoke. "Your words aren't as powerful as you think. How did you get back here?"

"The sheriff asked me where I wanted to go. He believed me. Jacob was a demon."

Crystal looked astonished. "It takes more than smooth talking for me to make up my mind about something."

* * *

Stabbing my best friend to death and dumping his body in a dumpster really squelched the reunion I was hoping to have. I'd imagined introducing all these *recovered* people from my past to all the hope-filled adventurers I planned to spend my future with. Instead, the group was huddled around a lonely fire listening to Crystal puke in the forest. Mosquitoes bit into us with the ferocity of miniature pit bulls.

I waited for sirens, for police cars to pull up at any moment. The asylum with its midnight screaming had seemed more serene.

There was nothing special about the way the flames leapt for a higher branch, or the way sap sizzled and cracked. Nothing special about the brisk night air or the two glassy-eyed German Shepherds lying at Darren's feet.

The people who stared deeply into this energy, however, were special. It was as if they were entranced by something in the fire no one else could see, perhaps a long-forgotten history or an equally grand future.

We believed different things, but met on common ground. Darren asked as much of us as Jesus had, to give up our lives as we knew them, and I agreed wholeheartedly. There was no American dream here. No white-picket fences and little houses in the suburbs. We did not push designer strollers with earsplitting designer children. We took no minivan tax write-off. We left it all to live in an abandoned Scout Camp in Fox, Alaska.

In New Orleans, I'd given Charlie, Darren's cell-phone number. Charlie called two weeks later to let us know we had a place in the world.

* * *

Enter emotion. The nights were filled with sex and weeping; the days, with a labor that made my bones feel brittle and my muscles ache.

When the camp was originally built in 1964, its four lodges, office, chapel and cafeteria were full of both promise and Boy Scouts ages thirteen to nineteen. It served as a base to teach young people new and exciting ways to experience the world. It was a crash-course on nature for children who found themselves miles from home, away from loved ones and mama's soothing voice. Of course they made friends; campers were mixed with other strange children and threatening adults. They formed alliances in case the adults suddenly turned on them, or the pasty-white redheaded kid made good on his threat to stick your head in the toilet.

It was not unlike what we were doing with our adult lives, adult jobs and adult reason. Only the taller-than-average bully who told us where to stick it was the world.

All this time, I wrote. Through war and torment, the pages unfolded and begged to be written on.

When this is over, I will have so little soul left that I ache to get as much down now as I can. I hope some poor, lonely soldier will glean a bit of hope or wisdom from these corrupt words. We all have at least one thing we can offer the rest. I hope to God this is a worthy offering, because I've spent all I had on it.

23 PREPARATION

I wept for Jacob daily, stopping in the middle of pouring concrete or painting to collapse in emotional convulsions. Sometimes, I wished I had been arrested and sent to prison to live out my days. It wasn't fair that Jacob should die while I lived on.

His family meant as much to him as mine had to me, yet our wives and children had faded from sight like mere illusions. They seemed like people we'd once known in dreams so sweet we wished we could fall back asleep and revisit them.

I'd wanted us to be a part of the same new family— something more solid than any domestic mirage.

* * *

I drove Darren's work-truck loaded with lumber. Daniel rode in the passenger's seat holding boxes filled with screws and nails. I gasped and slammed on the brakes. Nails flew, smashing and scattering on the floor of the cab.

A skeletal, fleshless demon appeared between two homes. It was massive even from a distance. Wings were folded behind its boney ribcage. The demon's wolf-like head stood taller than the surrounding buildings, its dark sockets robbed of eyes.

Daniel grabbed the dash to steady himself. "What's going on?"

I looked between the houses, up and down the block. I scanned the cloudless sky. "I saw something."

The demon had vanished.

"Are you okay? What did you see?"

"A demon."

Daniel looked shaken. He glanced outside the cab and then at me. "What are you talking about?"

I pressed on the gas, and the truck lurched ahead.

The demon remained hidden.

* * *

That night around the fire, I told the group what I'd seen.

"I believe you," said Rachael.

The others looked perplexed. I felt like Jesus returning to a roomful of Thomas'. They stole looks from each other, searching for a sign of what to believe.

"Part of our job is to protect people from demons," I said.

Their silence stung my pride and sanity. Crystal kept her distance.

Everyone looked as though they were screaming inside without moving their mouths. Crystal must have been shouting, "He killed his friend and threw him in a dumpster! He's insane!"

My eyes met hers. Her features softened by firelight. I felt she might fade away.

* * *

The idea was to build a place for reality to thrive. All we had to do is create something for others to join. Similar to a mega-church taking pledges and constructing a state-of-the-art worship facility. Only our pledges were our lives and our worship was our sweat.

We repaired roofs, electrical problems and constructed a sixty-five by thirty-foot A-frame greenhouse between the lodges and the lake. Victor and Daniel covered it with clear plastic. Matt, Rachael and I filled it with soil that smelled a thousand years old. We planted rows, hoping to have corn, potatoes, tomatoes and squash in a matter of months.

The lake held plenty of Dolly Varden and Bull Trout. We looked forward to a good year, growing and canning what we could, before the days grew dark.

I'd longed for a connection with nature since I was a child. I felt the sheer reality of the earth would complete me. I hiked to the lake's feeder stream where water had worn stones smooth over millennia. Salmon splashed and spawned in a struggle to fertilize and die. I scooped dirt—black as coffee grounds. Life squirmed, uncovered in my palm. All around, seeds exploded from their husks.

It was more than I could handle, as though I'd attempted to take a leisurely swim in a lagoon and been swept out to sea. Suddenly the water turned as murky and threatening as my unanswerable questions.

We step toward metaphor, lured by the transcendence it provides, longing to fill our stories with redemption and enlightenment.

I couldn't help but think that each person in the group was an animal making a place for themselves in the world—searching for where they fit.

Sometimes we embraced anger or lusted after each other's mates, but we never argued about politics or anything as intangible as which television shows to watch. Somehow, we were living in a more substantial place, with real anger and a love we dreamed would live on without us.

God seemed as real as my need to eat and drink. Things I'd questioned my entire life lay before me like platters filled with seasoned meats, cheeses and toasted breads.

Nothing matters without hope. However, true hope is expensive. "Pick up your cross and follow me." Without surrender no choice is made. One must weigh sacrifice against their quotient of faith.

I had faith that Crystal was my angel.

As her body and mind failed, she was forced to walk with a cane. She learned things unknowable by the rest of us and found her own sweet song to sing.

I watched her as we hauled cement, hammered nails, cleaned buildings and prepared meals.

Aidenn grew. We lived in Bohemian-style barracks, where eager teenagers used to sleep on their first stints away from home. We too were eager, but had trouble putting our finger on why or for what. It had something to do with purpose. We worked and planned, amazingly unified for all of our differences.

* * *

I was overjoyed. I'd spoken with Larry on the phone, and he'd decided to fly out and see us.

In a matter of weeks, he was sitting lakeside with the group in early morning. I'd thought it would be special to watch the sunrise, forgetting the sun never fully set.

Geese flew trumpeting. Water molecules swept off the lake and grassy chlorophyll filled our senses.

"This is beautiful country," said Larry.

Darren sharpened his knife, scraping a rectangular stone over the edge. "We've heard that you work with the homeless."

Larry nodded. "My partner Dougal and I started a not-for-profit some years back."

"They do good work," I said. "They help people overcome their demons."

"I do a lot of addiction counseling," said Larry.

Rachael, Matt and Daniel lay to one side, snapping reeds and twirling them between their fingers, making buzzing sounds. Dorothy rambled along the shoreline mumbling her prayers.

Jack and Marie Parker sat on lawn chairs as if waiting for a parade, but there was only Larry to watch, my overweight drug and alcohol counselor. Larry dressed as though we were meeting in a convention center, khakis now steeped in goose dung. His gray, hooded sweatshirt billowed about him where he sat.

"I was hoping Larry would counsel us while he's here," I said. "Help us fight some demons."

"You're the one who sees demons," said Marie. "Maybe *you* should meet with him."

"I will. So will you, if you know what's good for you."

"Are you threatening me, Brendan?"

"Just trying to help."

"Well . . . I'm not sure I need help from someone who hallucinates."

Darren took me by the arm. "Hold on, you two."

Everyone was paying attention now.

"No," I yanked my arm away. "I'm just saying, you'll see Larry if you know what's good for you. Unless you think you're better than the rest of us."

"I don't think I'm better. I just think some of us need help more than others."

I pointed at Daniel. "Daniel was there. Tell them."

Daniel shook his head. "I'm sure you saw what you saw."

"There. See." I got to my feet. "I saw a demon, same as before. Anyone who doesn't believe me can leave."

I looked at Larry, but couldn't read him.

"We're a family," said Darren. "We're in this together. No one can tell anyone to leave, any more than a brother or sister can say you're no longer family."

* * *

The grander our inner world, the more we hide its entrance. Trivial, freeing ideas lie on the ground there like fallen leaves highlighting the border of insanity. Tomorrow they will turn brown and die, but today they are gold and orange, red and yellow, awaiting the eyes of someone not afraid to look. Don't let this world of beauty die without first being adored. It may bring the all-encompassing hope we've been looking for.

God told us to approach him as though a child. The longer I live, the less I know about life. The deeper I dig, the less I know about myself. The profound is so close to the profane, and we knew both better as children.

* * *

Darren gathered us close at the water's edge and explained how the Chaco people had a road outside their spiritual center in New Mexico. It spanned thirty to forty miles and ended abruptly at a cliff. Explorers found thousands of pottery shards at the bottom. Sacrifices made from this world into the next. Breaking these pots made them unusable and transferred them to the afterworld. I feel many of us are already as unusable as shattered pottery. We have already decided what the purpose of this life is, and we may be wrong.

We long for the next stage, in which we will be truly born again. We spend our days in monotonous routine secretly hoping the rapture will occur, only fearing we may not be ready for such an event. Those who are certain they are ready are most surely not. They may be certain in their minds, but the mind and heart are so far apart. They span the distance of the road the Chacos used. We carry our pots and our hearts to the edge and break them, hoping to see a glimpse of the other side.

24 COMBINING WORLDS

Late at night, wolves haunted the world with howls from across the lake. They were in their own kind of pack, looking for food, leaning on each other, hungry for something they had not yet found.

I wished I could breach death's barrier and call to my wife and daughter or Jacob the way the wolves called to each other. I feared that in the effort, I might find my life cast off and shattered at the bottom of a cliff.

One of my father's sayings saved my life: "This too shall pass." It must have been a bit of what kept him going. It holds a promise made by nature herself: change is inevitable; how we perceive it is up to us.

We are meant to live in reality as it truly is. Morgues, suicide hotlines and asylums teem with men and women who have paid the steep price of opening the door and looking outside.

* * *

Darren and I sat alone in the cafeteria reading a newspaper. Everyone else had started their workday.

He folded the paper and slid it over. "Look at this."

The headline read: *Ice-Pick Killer Strikes Again.* I read on. A man from Beaver was found dead in his basement; his body slumped over a model railroad set. Puncture wounds were found on the back of his neck and head.

Similar victims were being found all over Alaska. A woman last to close a beauty shop was found sitting in a chair facing a mirror, bloody marks on the back of her head and neck.

A body was found in Lush Lake. "This attack seems to coincide with a string of murders we are actively investigating," explained Lead Investigator, Sheriff Burt Cobbs of Fairbanks.

The demon I'd seen in town fluttered though the caverns of my mind—a high-soaring shadow nearly beyond sight.

* * *

I met Crystal in Aidenn's new indoor garden. She looked at home kneeling and checking on the buds. Her hair dangled over her sprouting creations. The air was wet and heavy. Everything smelled of soil. She got to her feet.

I stood at the doorway. "Didn't I tell you this was a good place?"

She smiled and carried a watering can to the corn. "You did." Her leg shook. She struck it. "Damn it! I think it's getting worse."

I moved close. "Your hair smells like honey."

She nearly laid her head on my shoulder, but hesitated and pulled away.

"I think the murders all over Alaska are somehow tied to the demon I saw in town," I said.

Crystal's expression wilted. She knelt and poured water onto seedlings. "Sometimes I think this place would be more peaceful without you here." She eyed Matt and Daniel through the clear plastic wall. They were painting one of the lodges.

"Sometimes, I wonder if you're insane. I know you're smart. I know you have a vision. But some of the things you say. . ."

I reached for her hand, and she pulled away.

"The closer we get to true reality the more we'll agree," I said.

"Brendan, I don't think I'm ever going to believe demons are out there killing people."

"I'm just asking you to believe in possibilities," I said. "That's all I've ever asked of anyone. It's not my job to tell you what's real."

"Well, right now I'm dealing with the possibility that you're insane." She raised her trembling hands. "All of this seems crazy."

"Maybe, but we created it. It's real." I searched for the answer to the riddle behind her clear, blue eyes.

25 BELIEVING

Larry and I sat next to the lake under a lingering sun. It was ten in the morning, but could have been anytime.

My sanity floated high above like cheerful, white clouds, blowing into shapes discernable only by those in the mental health field.

Larry said I had a wholesome attitude compared to years earlier. He always saw the best in a person—the bits of God shoved down and hidden in someone's heart. It was these parts he talked to—a rare and useful gift that made him vulnerable to deception. His magic was his ability to spot a demon a mile away and confront it in no time.

"So how are things going for you here?" he asked, leaning back and reclining on his elbows.

I searched the lapping water for something other than the reflection of the sky. Wispy clouds rode on its shimmering olive surface. "Fine."

"What do you want to get from all this?"

"Peace." The word flew from my mouth like a dove from an opened cage.

Larry sat up. "What does peace mean to you?"

"I realized a long time ago that no matter what happens, you can choose whether it affects you or not. You're in control."

"You think having peace means you're in control?"

"Of course," I said.

"What do you think you're in control of?"

"Whether or not I react to something. Like the other day, I shouldn't have reacted to Marie."

"You're right. You shouldn't have reacted, but do you think Hitler was at peace?"

"Hitler? Probably not."

"But he had so much control. He ran an entire nation."

"That's not the kind of control I'm talking about."

"Control is control," said Larry. "It's a rule of life. Like water collecting in those clouds. Eventually, when they're full, it rains. That's nature. Remember what I taught you: natural rules go beyond what you can touch and see. Someone hungry for control eventually tries to force his will on others. It's a rule."

"So how do I find peace?"

Larry grinned. "Slay your demons."

I looked across the lake at the evergreen-lined foothills and then back to Larry. His eyes seemed both soothing and remorseless, like the caring expression of someone about to pull a trigger.

"Understand just how big nature is," said Larry. "We all have to play by the rules. People think they make different rules for themselves. They feel more comfortable that way. The universe is too big for them to wrap their heads around, so they play an entirely different game. In the end, we all bow to the same forces."

"None of this seems like a game to me," I said, "or if it is, I feel like I'm losing. No one but Rachael believes the demon I saw has anything to do with the murders. I'm getting tired of living in a world by myself."

"Ever since I met you, you've always lived in larger world. It's like the laws that govern the rest of us are just part of what you're working with."

"Isn't that the definition of insanity?"

"We all invite people into our worlds," said Larry. "Sometimes the more real the world is, the harder it is for people to accept the invitation."

"You think my world's real?"

"I know your world's real."

Not far away, a red and black bird skipped along a stump scanning the ground for bugs.

I looked across the expanse of shimmering water to the other side of the lake. "Sometimes I feel like we're all on our own islands, and people watch from shore as others try to reach them in boats."

Larry picked at the blades of grass. "The real question is: do you believe you're island is worth reaching?"

I paused and thought about my seminars where I preached a message of salvation through intercourse with the universe—being upfront and personal, letting real life course through your veins until it became part of you. "I think so. Some days I wonder."

"I think it is. That's why I'm here. I think I know you pretty well, Brendan. Does that scare you?"

"Why would that scare me?"

"People often fear what they want most, and I think you want to be reached."

A breeze blew from the northwest, across the lake and past us. The long grass leaned with it and wavered back to attention.

"I keep hoping that this place and these people are somehow the answer," I said. "But you know what? I don't think they are. I think we have to find our own answers."

"And what's your answer?" asked Larry.

"I think the answer has always been there, right in front of us. When I lost Jane and Ashley, I didn't just lose my wife and daughter, I lost a part of myself. I was a husband and father. For a while, I felt like a hero to these people, but that spell seems to be wearing off. I want to feel like a hero again, like my life means something for someone else, not just myself."

We spoke into the afternoon.

After which, Larry met with Dorothy, Jack and then Marie.

Larry was a potent drop of reality mixing with our psyches. Eventually, even the most cynical among us were drinking in his healing words.

I think we are so used to God's goodness, we no longer see it, even though proof surrounds us. Like Larry often said, "Proof changes nothing for an unbeliever."

* * *

Larry was a lot like me. He couldn't stop something once he'd begun it. He'd rescheduled his departure three times for the sake of seeing us through all he'd envisioned. He saw hope for our tattered lives—the best we could be—even when we couldn't see it in ourselves. I thought he was the best of men for it. I respected Darren in a similar way for seeing past three trailers and a fire ring and into the mansions growing in people's hearts.

"Have you ever heard of Lipan?" asked Darren, one day, as we ate baloney sandwiches together.

"No," I admitted, shaking concrete powder from my clothes.

"He was a general of old, commanding tens of thousands of soldiers in Asia Minor. He began in what is now known as Iran and conquered and enslaved many peoples.

"As the legend goes, one summer's day, when the breeze blew just right and perfectly balanced the heat of the day, and

167

bees flew from flower to flower in the fields outside Persepolis, four-thousand men marched and rode upon the city. Lipan had won every battle he'd been sent to, and his pride was swollen. He used far fewer men than were at his disposal and attacked in the light of day. He watched from a nearby hill as his forces were overwhelmed. Not one of them survived. He fled in defeat."

I took a bite of my sandwich and swallowed hard. "What happened?"

"The next morning, he was found poisoned in his tent with a note explaining why he had done himself in. The letter read, 'Since I was young and in my mother's care, I have sought out enemies to defeat. As I grew older and gained importance, I led ever-increasing numbers of soldiers and put down resistance wherever it could be found. Upon the deaths of my finest men, I was struck by the revelation: I am my own worst enemy. I must be put down with the same vengeance with which I have slain others. To fail to do so would throw everything I hold sacred into ruin. Forgive me.'

"Do you know why I'm telling you this, Brendan?"

"Why?"

"Because Lipan was greater than either of us."

* * *

As we were being counseled, taught and told about ourselves in unexpected ways, people were being murdered.

26 THE MONSTER IN THE MIRROR

I have no idea what the future holds, but I have every reason to believe there will be at least as many good times as bad. We see what we have to. This phenomenon has been the driving force behind a great many relationships, and perhaps even the backbone of our knowledge of God.

To survive, one must have the will to carry on. To have the will to carry on, one must have hope. Not a flimsy subjective hope either, but something that grounds us above all else—a faith. Something that puts a smile on a sad person's face and stores disillusionment away—neat and tidy—where one can return and observe it when the time is right.

A life with Crystal seemed like a lot to hope for, but maybe not too much.

* * *

The mirror in the cafeteria bathroom engulfed the entire room behind me. I stared into it and searched as deeply as possible into my own eyes, looking for my soul among the wreckage that lay in all I'd seen. I wondered if I could tell if I was a liar, the way I could tell others were liars, by simply looking into their eyes. I wondered if I could tell when I was to die, the way I could sometimes see death in others, even if it were some ways off. I thought I saw my own death, but maybe I was deceiving myself.

I was reminded of my uncle. I wondered what he had seen when he looked into his reflection—a man or something else.

We strive to be the men and women we grew up believing we'd be. If we're honest, we will admit we've fallen short, rejoiced in the failure of others and focused on such thoughts as little as possible.

Unbending rules, to which nature herself adheres, cover us like a sheet on a cadaver. However, we are free to hope beyond our own limits, as far as we can manage. Perhaps, in this act we may find a lost and determined child who is ready to grow up, tears for the right reasons and a sacred bravery.

* * *

That night, I listened to the group sleep in their sections of the lodge. Their snoring sounded like pigs in a mud bath. My reflection haunted me.

I slid close to Crystal and whispered, "Are you awake?"

She stirred. "What?"

"I'm sorry." I spoke my words into the dark, not sure where they might fall.

"For what?"

"What we talked about the other day—me being crazy." I felt the pressure of tears building. "It's just that I've always been someone who sees more than others, even when I was a child. I can't help it."

Crystal reached her hand out from under the blankets and sought me out. She stroked my arm.

I collapsed onto the floor beside her. "You're all I've ever dreamt of. You know that, don't you?"

She pulled her hand back. "Stop saying that. You shouldn't say stuff like that, unless you mean it."

I looked for her features and saw only darkness. "Of course I mean it."

"You don't even know me."

"That's not true. I know you."

"Then tell me. What's the most important thing to me? Not what do *you* wish was important to me. What *is* important to me? Do you even know?"

I thought and then rambled off a list. "Pottery, gardening, children?"

Crystal lay as motionless as Jane had when I visited her underground.

Then I heard the soft sniffles of her crying. She shook in sobs. "Why does it have to be like this? Why can't things just be easy for once? Why does life have to be so Goddamn hard?" She pounded her fist on the concrete floor. "I wanted to have a family," she sniffed. "Do you think this is easy for me? You bring me to this Godforsaken nut farm with all these promises, kill your friend on the way and now you expect me to be your lover?"

I listened. There was far less snoring. "I want to have a family, too. We have a lot of the same dreams."

"Well, I can't, Brendan. This fucking disease has probably robbed me of that."

I had no idea what to say.

Crystal said, "When I first met you, I thought I knew who you were."

"People live with each other for years thinking they know who someone is," I said, "and one day they come home to find the person they thought they were going to grow old with dead on the floor."

"Yeah, well, that's happening faster for some of us."

I searched out her hand. She relaxed at my touch. "I don't want this to be about desperation," I said. "I want this to be about life."

"How can this be about life when I'm almost—"

I stopped her words with my lips. "Believe. All we need is belief to make this happen."

"Believe in what?"

"Believe in us. Believe in what's going on here."

"What is going on here?"

"Something wonderful. You're going to have to find out for yourself."

She looked away, further in the dark. I held her chin and gently turned her head, seeing only darkness but imagining a loving stare.

* * *

Something scratched outside near dawn. I could hear it through the windows that lined the upper part of the wall. I fell paralyzed, afraid to get my knife, because of Jacob.

I squeezed out the door into the frigid night. Fog hung. Frogs croaked and splashed. Crickets chirped far-off near the lake.

I heard the shriek too late. Something cracked onto my skull. I fell to my knees, then lay semiconscious reaching to the back of my head. My scalp wet. My hair matted from the blood oozing from the gash. I staggered to my feet, attempted to stand and collapsed onto the ground again.

"Oh, my God." Dorothy stood over me with a plumbing wrench in her hand. "You scared the shit out of me. I thought you were that demon thing you keep talking about. . . . The well is leaking again." She leveraged the wrench so that it landed in the palm of her other hand. "Are you bleeding?"

"I'll be all right," I said. But I wouldn't be. I'd have a ringing in my head until the day I died. At least, that's what the doctor said.

Pieces snapped together in the waiting room. I realized something amongst the TV news ramblings, the piped-in Muzak, the diseased air and the three-kilohertz buzz between my ears. Reporters had tailed Burt Cobbs and surrounded his car to get the scoop on the thirteen-year-old girl who'd been deemed the Ice-Pick Killer's sixth victim. Rhonda sat next to the perturbed Sheriff, shielding her face from one camera and looking into another.

I thought back to the times I'd seen the two together, and wondered if she'd told him my secret about the pyramid. Had he told her to leave me and hide at the motel? What else had the two of them planned?

27 REALITY HUNTER

There are people who spend their lives tracking vampires that supposedly live in the caves of coastal cities around the world, or purchase boats, sonar equipment, or submarines in pursuit of legendary aquatic dinosaurs. I began to wonder if these people, scoffed at by so many, including myself, were on to something. Were they experiencing "reality" while you and I were dumb and numb to it all, sleeping soundly in our presumptions? Did these people see what they were after as clearly as I saw the monsters in my own life?

The only nemeses I had were demons, but they were enough. There was an entire underworld crawling with them. They were as real as anyone's imagination or dysfunction, as solid as any relationship, addiction, or prayer. You couldn't tell me they didn't exist and no one tried anymore.

* * *

Under the guise of picking up supplies, I drove the truck past town and down half of the long unpaved driveway leading to Burt Cobb's home. I parked and trudged the rest of the way to arrive unnoticed.

Rhonda's dusty Escort was parked in front of the house, to the side of the garden, smelling of gasoline. Painted stones and the brown plastic rabbit hinted of previous joyous times when the weedy beds may have thrived with seasonal flowers. This is where I'd found the butterfly.

Through the front window, I saw Rhonda pacing inside. I sneaked around to the back of the house to look for a way in and heard the most ghastly moans and thuds coming from behind the cellar doors. Time suspended. The white, double doors thumped with such force, I expected them to explode open at any moment.

Instinct told me what was behind them, but I hadn't trusted my instincts since Jacob's death.

I stepped closer. Boards bent outwards ready to snap. Steel braces held them. A demon spoke in a deep, wistful voice, "Brendan, let me out."

A chill ran the length of me. I knew this voice. A similar voice spoke to me at my home when Jane and Ashley first disappeared and at the asylum when Rhonda received her thrashing.

The first of the pins holding the door eased its way out of its cylinder, clanged against the wood and rolled onto the dirt below. I watched helplessly, even though it was the pickax in my hand that had un-lodged the pin. The door creaked open from the top. Long, skeletal fingers flashed from inside.

"Now the other one." The words rang above the buzz in my head.

"What are you doing?" screamed Rhonda. She stood at the side of the house.

The doors exploded open and a flood of people crawled and staggered from the cellar, breathing heavily and squinting in the light. Most shielded their eyes from the sun. These people weren't right. Their skin clung tight as if they were walking skeletons. Their heads were fleshy skulls with eyes.

Rhonda's hands were on her head. She mouthed the words, "Oh, my God," then ran back to the front of the house.

Two of the creatures turned on me, as the others stumbled into the surrounding forest, their skin and eyes jaundiced. I ran with them on my heels. I wanted to break into tears, but instead tightened my grip on the pickax's handle.

A man and a woman demon, both with mangled shirts and slacks, stood just outside the forest line. I peered from behind a tree.

"You're coming with us," groaned the woman.

"You're my hero," said the man in a drool-dripping mock.

"Back off," I said. "I'm not going with anyone."

Smiles hatched on their faces like maggots. They hunted me, one on either side.

I wound up the ax like a player with a bat. "Back off!"

They were on me at once, burning my skin. I swung the ax into the man's leg. He screamed, grabbed the weapon and threw it to the side. There was a gunshot. We turned. Rhonda stood on the edge of the forest wielding a shotgun. I hobbled and grabbed the ax, bleeding everywhere I'd been touched. The man held his leg, but had no blood.

"Get over here," yelled Rhonda.

I obeyed.

The woman charged with a shriek, waving her arms. Rhonda shot a deafening blast. The woman tumbled to the forest floor. The man swore and ranted, holding his leg.

Rhonda pumped the shotgun. "Burt will be here soon."

We locked the man back in the cellar.

* * *

Burt, Rhonda and I met in Burt's arts-and-crafts living room, fifteen minutes later.

Burt barked inches from my face. "What the hell did you think you were doing?"

"I don't know," I admitted. "You had a cellar full of possessed people. What were *you* doing?"

Burt paced the room. "Well, they're out now, thanks to you."

"What's going on here?" I asked.

Rhonda gestured to a seat on the couch beside her. "What do you remember?"

"What do you mean? What am I supposed to remember?"

"Do you remember doing this to me?" She pulled the clothes off her shoulders and back, exposing deep red scars.

I put my head in my hands. "I never did that."

"Not the you that's with us now," she said. "But that's not the only *you* there ever was."

"I don't understand."

Burt placed his hand on his gun. "You can't remember, because you're possessed."

"Was possessed," corrected Rhonda.

"I'm not so sure," said Burt. "Why did he let the others out?"

"I knew there was a demon inside," I said. "I was going to kill it."

"Well, you didn't," said Burt.

"I realize that," I said. "What were you going to do with those people?"

Burt took on a granite disposition. He looked out the window, at the grass and trees alive with sunlight and fresh air.

Rhonda got up from the couch, coasted to her man and slid her hand onto his arm. "Burt's protecting people."

I shook my head. "I don't remember hurting you."

"It was in the institution." She re-clothed her shoulders.

"Follow me," said Burt, "I want to show you something."

He took me to a staircase in the kitchen, opened a door at the bottom and said, "Go ahead."

The cellar was as dark as deep space. Rhonda agonized at the top of the stairs. She was the last thing I saw as the light collapsed around me and the door locks clicked. My nerves shattered and knees weakened. How could I have been so stupid as to walk into this? He was in here, somewhere.

I listened for breathing and heard only my own. I beat on the thick wood of the door with all my might. "Let me out. I'm not a demon."

I was grabbed from behind by the ankles. My legs blistered and bled. I kicked until I landed a solid blow, threw my leg into the air and missed.

My ankles seared like coals. "I know you're there. I know I hurt you, you bastard."

Suddenly, I was on the floor, my hands protecting my face. He was on top, holding my wrists. They blistered at his touch.

A light was born in the middle of the room. A pyramid covered with symbols. The man stuttered a scream. His face melted like hot wax. His body went limp. I threw him to the side, where he thrashed and burst into flames. In a matter of minutes, only a charred mark remained. The pyramid's glow pulsed like a heartbeat. The smell was fricasseed death. Burnt spots marked the entire room. The pyramid snapped off. The bolt turned and door swung open. Rhonda and Burt's eager faces met with mine.

"We had to be sure," said Burt.

I wanted to punch him, but knew I didn't stand a chance in a fight. So, I accepted Rhonda's congratulatory hug and limped upstairs after them.

I sat on the couch and cuffed the remainder of my jeans exposing searing sores. "What the hell just happened?"

Burt put his pistol into its holster. "You're not a demon."

"And you're not on your way to becoming a demon," said Rhonda.

Burt looked tense. "I've had totally normal looking people blow up on the inside."

"I already told you," I said.

"We had to be sure," said Burt.

"That was loads of fun. You'll have to have me over again sometime!" I dabbed my wounds with my jeans.

"We should get you something," said Rhonda. "You're bleeding."

"These were my only good pair," I said.

Rhonda smiled and tromped up the stairs.

I knew what she was thinking. She was thinking, "Wow, I really miss your sense of humor. And I'm stuck here with this Blue Blocker-wearing son of a bitch who burns people alive."

God, you just can't win, I thought. You try and find a normal guy.

Burt took a seat on the edge of a Lazy Boy. "We need you to help us round those fine citizens back up."

Fuck you, I thought.

"What about your deputies?"

"This isn't exactly legal, if you hadn't noticed," said Burt.

Rhonda returned with a box of first-aid supplies and prepared gauze.

I mourned, remembering the relationship that was once mine and Rhonda's. "It's hard to believe there isn't a better way. These are *people*."

Burt lit a pipe he'd snatched off the mantel. The fragrance of black-cherry tobacco drifted across the room. "Not anymore. They're scum. People with demons are demons, and you just let them out."

Rhonda stretched white ribbons round my ankle. "You were always talking about how you'd like to kill your demon."

I winced. "Yeah, but if someone's possessed, they can be exorcised."

"That only lasts so long," said Burt, letting smoke seep from his lips. "Once someone's possessed long enough, they change physically.

"Not long after my wife passed, I got a call to come down to the station. One of the guys we'd incarcerated was flipping out. We called the doctor to give him some sedatives and went into the cell with four deputies. That doctor's still got a hand print on his face where he was burned."

"What happened to the guy?"

"We kept him in there. He started turning yellow and looking really sick. I have to be honest. We didn't do anything about it, because he'd sent two of my deputies to the hospital. He stayed in the corner of the cell covered with a blanket for days. We called to him and he didn't answer. He hardly ate. When we finally investigated, what we uncovered wasn't human. It was what those things downstairs were becoming."

"What happened to it?"

"We shipped it to Anchorage. It's in the psych ward at Alaska Regional."

I shook my head. "I doubt it."

Burt tapped his spent tobacco into a clay bowl. "And why's that?"

"I've seen these things disappear through some sort of spiritual door. At some point, they're not confined by the physical world anymore. We're not just dealing with the rules we understand here."

Burt nodded and bit his cheek. "That explains it. I've had several of them disappear on me. We've got to stop them."

Jack Carris floated to the surface of my thoughts, the way he'd disappeared from work. The rules changed. No one remembered him. I wondered if he could have had a demon.

28 CONVINCING OTHERS

The cafeteria was bathed in comforting smells and sounds: eggs popping over grease, processed bacon and sausage, bread toasting. Once, like Pavlov's dog, this triggered salivation, but now announced the workday.

Rachael and Matt sat next to Larry. Jack and Marie Parker ratcheted sausage links into their mouths. Darren, Daniel, Victor, Dorothy and Crystal sat further down.

I stood at the head of the table visiting each of their faces. "I know some of you are going to have a hard time with this, but demons are real."

They looked under-whelmed, as though what I was saying wasn't a revolutionary concept but something you might hear the homeless muttering from a park bench.

"I'm serious," I said.

"Brendan, we've all talked about this," said Darren. "We concluded that it's fine for you to believe in demons as long as you respect our beliefs. And, we don't."

A tree fell in my inner-forest, but no one heard it. "So, let me understand this. You are all following my teachings, but you don't believe me?"

"There's more to life than what one person says," said Marie. "Just the other day, I bought this book on eating for your blood type and . . ."

"We *are* following your teachings," said Dorothy.

Rachael pushed her plate away. "Didn't you tell us that our inner worlds are every bit as important as our outer worlds?"

"I did."

"Well, aren't all of our inner worlds different?"

Marie interrupted, "When I was a little girl we didn't talk about stuff like that."

"No," I said. "I think the same rules that define reality apply to everybody."

"We need to get started with the day," Darren announced. "Who's got cleanup duty today?"

Victor and Jack raised their hands. The group got up and grabbed their trays, anxious for a chance to leave.

"Brendan's right," said Larry.

People stopped and perked their ears.

"Brendan said, 'Demons are real.' And they are."

"No they're not," said Marie.

"Each of us has demons we have to battle in our lives," said Larry. "That's all I've done since I got here, help each of you battle your demons. That's all I do in the city."

Victor stroked his beard. "When Brendan's been saying demons, he means demons in our lives."

Everyone nodded tentatively.

"No," I said. "I'm talking about the physical world."

Half the room sighed.

Darren motioned to me. "I think I should have a talk with Brendan alone."

"No, damn it! You all need to listen. The only reason this place exists is because of my teachings, and I'm telling the truth. You can build this place and invite people here and have your little cult, but—"

"That's enough, Brendan!" Darren shouted.

"No. It's not enough!"

"This isn't a cult," yelled Rachael.

"Yeah," replied some others.

"It will be if you don't understand and teach the truth."

"And what's the truth?" asked Victor. "That there're real demons running around out there?"

"Yes," I said.

"I'm willing to believe a lot," said Darren, "but—"

"What are you saying?" asked Matt. "Where are these demons?"

Larry held up his hand. "Brendan suffers from schizophrenia."

The group fell silent, and I along with them.

Larry's eyes looked gentle, even as he thrust the blade of his words into my gut. "He sometimes has episodes."

I curled up my pant leg and tore off the gauze, exposing the oozing, red handprints. "Does this look like an episode to you? I'm begging you all. Come to Sheriff Cobb's house. He'll explain everything we need to do."

* * *

It's strange how what drives us may abandon us midstream, how what tickles our ears with lies one moment may tell us truths that knock us on our emotional ass the next.

After all, it is an unbelievably real world, with Darwin scribbling his thoughts into books and telling us what monkeys we are. Each of us explores possibility, hungry for sustaining adoration, yet we know enough to render ourselves helpless.

We strive and strain, bellow and believe, we learn, and everything we learn tells us the same thing: life is one great meaningful experience in a meaningless world. Brilliance has many parts, yet each part is incomplete.

We live, heal and attempt to piece together a picture worth the price of our very lives.

The picture I saw presented demonic executioners, who crippled those daring to look and consumed souls without defense. They're everywhere. Some are people we know. Others are the great fears and addictions of our lives.

* * *

Later that day, we packed ourselves into Burt's living room and listened to something hammer in the basement. Everyone exchanged glances, as though we were children committing sins.

Burt had caught one, and it's rare for something to die without a fight.

We were all there, including Crystal and Rhonda, huddling in a stranger's home, waiting to be told just how vast and dangerous the real world was—the larger world we'd all been searching for.

Dorothy looked at the floor. "What's making all that noise?"

Burt looked at me, then at the group. "What did he tell you to get you here?"

Darren cleared his throat. "Brendan told us you knew something about demons."

Burt laughed. "Do any of you believe?"

A symphony of smacks and crashes sounded under our feet.

Burt pulled his revolver from its holster. "Follow me, if you want to."

Everyone marched into the kitchen. Burt descended the stairs, unlatched a series of locks and swung the door open, revealing a dark room. A fluorescent light snapped on. The creature cowered in a corner.

Alone in the dark, beating on the door, the menace had seemed powerful, but now it hid, as though it knew what it was. Searing, black eyes peered from a sickly yellow face.

I recalled reading a newspaper article about a father who'd raped both his son and daughter for years, with his wife's help. She would lead them into the bedroom wearing school uniforms.

When the parents were caught and brought before the court, the man shook to his core. The judge said he was not fit to be part of society, and sentenced him to death.

Burt threw the switch. The demon rolled and shuddered, spat and hissed, until a flame shot from it. The group watched, repulsed and wide-eyed.

Like the blue skies outside the slaughter plant, once we looked, we could never go back. The scene tainted us for life with gurgled screams and smoldering anguish.

Burt closed the door. The following was written on a piece of cardboard duct-taped to the back of it:

1. You see what you want to.

2. What you desire may not be beneficial.

And in large, red letters:

WATCH THE VIDEO IN THE VCR
BEFORE OPENING THIS DOOR!

Once in the living room, Burt rewound the tape in the VCR and pressed play. "I can't tell you how many times I've heard noises in the basement and came back up to watch this tape."

The screen sputtered, hissed and flashed. A grainy picture flicked on, showing a younger, less-frazzled version of Burt. The video explained the way feeding on hate, selfishness and fear erodes a person into an empty, destructive shell, until they are eventually a demon. "Flip the switch before you go in and whatever you do, don't believe a word they say." The screen snapped to static and white noise.

"I had to make this so I wouldn't forget what I was doing here," said Burt. "Some are better at it than others, but all demons have the power to make you forget and distort what you're thinking. Whatever you do, don't believe them. You might as well be talking to the devil."

Everyone looked as off-kilter as I was the first time one had approached me in my bedroom.

"What do you want from us?" asked Marie, before anyone else could. "What can *we* do?"

"We need to round them up," said Burt, without hesitation, as if we were cowhands and he was John Wayne on horseback.

"Round them up?" repeated the others.

29 A HEALTHY PERCEPTION

There's no way around our broken decisions, inherited demons, great lapses in character or hopeful futures. Our souls are mortal.

We can't cure the world. Sometimes, we can't even fix ourselves. But, whatever we find that needs repair must be mended with urgency. Who will heal the body or spirit other than themselves? If we're not self-healing, what is left but to die?

Each of us had spent countless nights around campfires discussing the purpose of life. Then, when meaning burst into our lives and crippled our version of the world, our instinct was to flee or ignore reason altogether.

* * *

The group returned home that night, heads filled with insane plans that seemed achievable and feelings that fell in torrents and muddied the paths of our ideas. Crystal and I watched the rest far off near the fire ring. I knew they must be making declarations of war against enemies they did not understand.

The air off the lake was dead, as if a fierce storm was mounting. The world glowed with yesterday's light. Even the crickets' chirps seemed dim.

Crystal pierced me with blue eyes, a sudden glance that stilled my heart. "I believe you. I think demons could be real, and the thought of them scares me more than anything."

Her words built a tower within me. I slid my hand around her waist and squeezed her tight. We looked out across the water, watching the subtle rise and fall of its surface.

A single butterfly fluttered into view, its vivid blue and yellow wings creased the gloom. It jittered in the air toward us like a fantastic omen. A million more followed, like flowers showering the sky. They flew around us like pleasant memories.

"Brendan?"

I blinked and they were gone, disappearing like a good day.

I looked at Crystal. Her pale skin shone, as though she were young enough to start her life over.

"What is it?" she asked.

"I'm just glad somebody finally believes."

The hope of having a new family overtook me. If someone believed in me, perhaps I could find the nerve and resources to believe in myself. Perhaps not the me that Crystal knew, or the me the others first saw and followed when they thought I held the answers to the mysteries of life, but the real me, dangling precariously from the truths I'd learned, ransomed with golden insights I'd found along the way.

I wondered how much like God I was, how much God was like us, and if who we sometimes believed in was really the Creator at all.

Crystal's leg shook. She punched it. "Damn it."

Love's not clean. True life is loving someone who shits their pants. True romance is doing the laundry and dishes.

I took Crystal's trembling hand and drew her close. "What matters more than holding the hand of someone you love?"

Sometimes, a loved one completes the work of art of our life. Analogy and metaphor bring reality into focus. They unite the profundity of God with mowing the lawn or washing the car. Everything is symbolic and symbiotic.

There is no way to meet our own needs unless we meet the needs of others and no way to meet other's needs unless we sustain our own. In this way, we are one and see things as one.

The irrelevant becomes relevant, the disconnected becomes wholly important and we become wise with insane thoughts.

* * *

Darren studied by candlelight while the group slept. Letters shone on pages, illuminated by the flame. The sharp contours of his face appeared even more rigid. His German Shepherds lay at his feet. They raised their heads and sniffed the air as I approached. "Finding anything useful?"

"This was the strangest day of my life," he said.

I took a seat nearby. "Welcome to my world. It takes some getting used to."

"I don't think I want to ever get used to watching someone burst into flames like that."

"It helps if you don't look at them as a person."

"You mean like the Nazis looked at the Jews during World War II?"

"Yeah, kind of like that."

"Take a look at this." Darren handed me a brown leather book and pointed to an entry. The book was entitled *Understanding the Real World*, by Norman Schrader.

I read the following: *"One may believe for this reason that the fabric of reality is woven with indisputable truths and laws that govern the world, and that these are imparted through knowledge and experience into the minds of men. The truth is found for us, however, from the insights of our ancestors. There was undoubtedly a time when early man first grasped the idea of good and evil. They may have peacefully gathered around a fire and set to eating the day's kill. One may have taken a larger portion for himself. Another responded with a blow to the greedy one's head and before long it became apparent how the world worked. It boiled down to perceivable gain and loss.*

"Though these concepts may have started in the visible world, they quickly evolved to include the intangible. Gain and loss deepened man's understanding and broadened the world in which he lived, when he began to interpret the things that happened to him in terms of morality.

"It was no longer simply theft or murder that could be perceived as loss, but the feelings and actions of hatred, un-forgiveness and insult. Each of which has a necessary and contradictory meaning. This is by design. The designer is still up for debate, but there is no question of how our minds work. In order to perceive the intangible concepts of gain, good, love, forgiveness and praise, there must be the antonyms loss, evil, hate, un-forgiveness and insult. Each of these sets present a conceptual spectrum necessary for perception. Suffice it to say, we need no opposite for a chair because it is tangible, but for wisdom we need folly. We need one to know the other and every discernable possibility in between.

"One question worth examining is whether good and evil exist beyond the minds of men, or if every concept is simply a coping mechanism for man's existence and evolution."

I closed the book and looked at Darren in amazement. "We're making it all up."

Darren gave a slow, understanding nod.

I felt the spine of the book in my hands. "This is amazing. This is the key."

Darren reached for the book. "I don't know that I'd go that far."

I held up my hand in protest, not ready to let it go. "I would. This explains everything." I said this louder than intended, and some snorers snorted in the darkness of the lodge.

"Like what?"

"We made it all up."

"Made what up?"

"Love and hate, good and evil, angels and demons!" I could tell he didn't get it. I barely understood myself. "There's the physical reality, right?" I motioned at the room.

"Right."

I threw up my hands. "We made up the rest."

"The rest of what?"

"Everything! Mankind made up a version of reality we could all live in. We're taught a lot of regurgitated ideas as children."

"Ideas that hold society together," said Darren matter-of-factly.

"Some of them," I said, "but the question is whether any of it exists without us."

"The proverbial tree falling in the forest." Darren grew in understanding.

"Yeah. Science tells us that sound waves travel when a tree hits the ground, but what about the rest of the rules, the rules that don't apply to the physical world, the rest of reality?"

"Are those the rules that Larry's always talking about?" asked Darren.

"Yeah, like how do we know when someone does something evil?"

"What do you mean?"

"Just like in the book, say someone hits you for no reason or because they're angry about something, and it's unjustified, whatever *that* means. Is that evil?"

"You mean I did nothing to them?" asked Darren.

"Yeah. You were walking down the street minding your own business and they haul off and punch you. Would that be evil?"

Darren nodded. "Yeah, that would be evil."

"How do you know?"

He paused for a moment. "Because I didn't provoke him?"

"Sounds logical, but how do you *really* know?"

"What do you mean?"

"How do you know if you provoked him or not?" I asked.

"Because in your example I was walking down the road minding my own business, and *he* hit *me*."

"What if you provoked them and didn't know it, or what if they only *perceived* that you provoked them?"

"Where are you going with this?" asked Darren. "Eventually there's got to be a reasonable way to deal with this kind of scenario."

"Reasonable? Don't tell me the lawyers are holding the fabric of reality together with their *reasonable* this and their *reasonable* that."

Darren shrugged. "I have no idea what you're getting at. You're starting to sound like Marie."

"That's uncalled for," I said. "My point is that if reality boils down to what's 'reasonable' for some, there's no sure way to tell if something's real or not. Other than a bunch of people getting together and agreeing on the best version of reasonable, and that's not reality. And, if I think demons are real or angels for that matter, and you don't think that's reasonable, who's right?"

"The one whose reality proves to be true . . . in the physical world," said Darren.

"So prove there's love."

"I can see love in the world through people's actions," said Darren.

"But can you see love itself?"

"Sometimes, I think I can. I got involved helping out at an orphanage in Honduras a few years back. I saw joy on those kids' faces every time they were handed a meal—a bowl of rice and sausage. I'd never seen or felt that much love before. Giving those kids anything was like giving a dying man another day."

"The same way you saw love," I said. "I see demons. We all can."

"But, I don't want to."

"Then that explains it. Remember the sign: You see what you want to."

* * *

Sunlight pierced the easterly windows. Eggs and bacon masked the smell of the burning flesh we carried in our noses from the previous evening. The group ate at long tables.

Darren took the posture of Moses making a speech. "I'd like to apologize to Brendan for not believing him."

Heads bowed and the group muttered apologies.

"We stayed up researching last night," Darren continued, "and we believe we know what's happening to these people."

"The things we hate and fear become us," I said.

Everyone stared, as though I'd just announced that the cyanide-laced Kool-Aid was to be served.

"What are you talking about?" asked Larry. "That doesn't make any sense. Fear and hate are emotions."

"Isn't that what Brendan's been saying all along?" asked Rachael. "Our inner world is every bit as real as our outer world."

"Maybe for an individual," said Larry. "But we're talking about reality here."

"We *are* talking about reality," I said. "And what's real for you is real for me, because we agree on it, and because of laws we have no choice but to obey. The laws *you* talk about."

We explained what we'd learned the best we could and the group grew quiet, as though what we were saying made sense, but at an unreachable level. They fidgeted about like children during a church service, hearing words but not understanding the implications.

"Larry, do you remember when you first counseled Jacob and me all those years ago?" I asked. "Internally, it was as if we were in a war together, and I was fighting alongside other men, for my family and my own sanity. To me, you were a wizard performing magic.

"For me, working for Charlie at the modeling agency in New Orleans was like working in a wax museum. The people there were like statues that had no minds of their own. Revisiting Club Seven was like walking into the bowels of hell, a breeding ground for my addictions."

Larry grabbed me by the arm with his comforting hand. "I'm proud of you for walking the path of sobriety, Brendan. But, you've got to realize that you have a unique way of looking at all of this. It isn't the world we're all in."

"It *is*, though. Reality's a shared perception, and I just shared it. Love and hate, good and evil, these are all agreed-upon ideas." I looked around the cafeteria at the group's unsettled faces. "It's the same thing we're doing here, building a place for people to be more real in, only it's all up here." I tapped on my head with a finger.

"You shared the idea, not the perception," said Larry.

"If we don't perceive a concept it doesn't exist for us," I said, "like a song doesn't exist for a deaf man, no matter how many times you play it. But we can all hear the song in his head if he sings it. I've always felt like a man singing a song that people needed to hear."

Their faces quickened with understanding.

"We're all singing our song, trying to get someone to listen," said Victor.

"When you think about it," I said, "there are at least as many realities as there are people: Christ's reality, Buddha's reality, Jack's reality, Marie's reality. Ultimately, we choose to share the same reality, because we don't want to be alone."

Darren placed a stack of books on the table and selected one. "We think Larry is playing a larger role in this than we'd realized. He's the one who's been helping us face our fears." Darren flipped through the book until he found what he was looking for, a picture of a wizard battling a large, red, fiery dragon. "One of the things we noticed last night is that whenever there's a demon or monster, the person's alone." Darren held up the picture for everyone to see.

"I don't think that means someone can't help fight once it shows up," I said. "Only that demons appear when a person's alone."

"Burt was by himself yesterday when he captured the demon," said Darren.

"Jack and I were talking," said Marie. "This is all a bit much for us. We liked things early on. When we were planning and building a peaceful place for people—a place to enlighten people's souls."

"Without the distractions of the world," added Dorothy.

"This isn't a monastery," said Victor. "The whole reason I got involved and went to the seminars in the first place was because I was looking for something. I didn't know what it was, but I was hoping someone would tell me."

"Same here," said Matt. "I feel like we're on the verge of something super big here."

"We just didn't plan on getting mixed up with a murder," said Marie. "Especially something like we saw yesterday. That was horrible. It took everything I had not to go to the police."

"He is the police," said Darren.

"That's what I mean," said Marie with a shudder. "That's how screwed up this is."

"It isn't murder if they're not a person," I said.

"But how can they not be a person?" asked Dorothy.

"We only see glimpses of the entire picture," I said.

"That's what we've spent the last year learning," said Rachael. "How we're not seeing it all."

"I think I see reality just fine," said Marie. "Until that guy burned up yesterday, I thought things were pretty good."

"You can't deny something just because you want to," said Rachael.

"I'm certainly not going to deny a murder," said Marie.

"It isn't murder if they're not a person," I said. "Many of you are on the verge of understanding something few people ever grasp."

"Reality isn't what we think it is," explained Darren. "It's bigger."

I kept glancing to Larry, who was nestled between Rachael and Daniel. He looked both contemplative and disturbed.

"So what is reality?" asked Victor.

"What Larry's been teaching us," said Darren. "The way to deal with any fear is to face it. Isn't that one of the rules?"

Larry adjusted his shirt collar. "It is."

"That makes sense," said Rachael. "But, what are we supposed to do? I don't want to face those things alone."

"Neither do I," echoed some others.

* * *

We reported to Burt Cobb's home with our perceptions as tattered as flags after a war. The apparitions of magnificent worlds danced in the corner of our eyes, but when we looked, they wafted away. The secret we were learning was that the

196

world we shared was built with nothing more than the brick and mortar of our ancestors' imaginations. Things existed because we needed them to.

What Jesus said was true. With a mustard seed of faith, you *can* move mountains, especially if these were mountains of your own creation.

We didn't know exactly how demons spread, but they did. Every man, woman and child was susceptible to desperately evil intentions. This left them open to parasitic attack. Yet, illuminated angels could be found in the most unlikely of places—at the carwash, the supermarket or cleaning the bathroom of your motel room.

The more I grasped and the deeper I dug, the more I saw that the real world was larger than I'd ever believed. Eventually, we saw not only demons and angels for what they were, or the world for what it is, we saw ourselves with both our frightening and joyful identities. We saw evidence of a nameless God, whose personality eludes us, making rules that every reality shares.

* * *

We wandered through the Sheriff's home. Burt stepped out of the kitchen holding several newspapers. The headlines showed that the Ice-Pick Killer had been busy. There were murders happening all over Alaska, many of them committed without an ice-pick.

"We have to stop them," said Burt. "I'm working with many police departments, but very few officers are going to see these things for what they really are."

"So how do we find them?" asked Matt.

Darren joined me on the couch.

"Mine has always found me," I said.

Burt paced. "I just go to places I think demons might be: alleys, bars, graveyards, those kinds of places, but every once in a while I'll see someone in a grocery store or walking down the street, and I just know. Something inside tells me."

"Larry can see them," I said. "He can spot a demon a mile away. How do you do it?"

"It's hard for me to believe that someone's fear or hate physically changes them," said Larry. "The demons I look for are addictions and unhealthy behaviors."

"I'd say killing someone's a pretty unhealthy behavior," said Burt.

"I've been seeing my demon for years," I said.

"I know you have," said Burt, "longer than any of us."

"I think I get it," said Matt. "Truth is truth, whether it's inside someone or a part of a greater reality."

"Greater reality." I laughed. "Wars are fought over whose reality is greater."

"Does everyone remember why they're here?" asked Burt.

There were a series of yeses and nods.

"Damn, that means they're leaving town."

"Where are they going?" asked Rachael.

"Wherever they damn well please," said Rhonda, under her breath.

Burt paced. "I've never dealt with a group this big. They'll unite and find a leader."

"Maybe we ought to wait 'til dark," said Rhonda. "Isn't that when they come out?"

Burt stopped. "I'm hoping to get a jump on them before they kill again."

I got to my feet. "I wonder if the Ice-Pick Killer was the demon I saw in town?"

"What demon?" asked Burt.

"I saw it a couple weeks ago. It was huge and had wings."

"We didn't believe him," said Dorothy.

"You should have told me," said Burt.

Darren stood. "If those things are out there killing people, I don't think we should be in here talking. We should break into teams and track the bastards down."

The demon had revealed itself in the light of day, as if it had nothing to hide. I imagined it wallowing in the sewer system, grunting and seeking out its next victim or flying high above, soaring on filthy wings.

Burt and Rhonda spread out a map on the coffee table. "I've sectioned up areas around where each attack occurred," said Burt. "I need volunteers for each one."

"How can we possibly cover that much area?" asked Victor.

Burt looked over the map. "We have no choice."

"That's not reasonable," said Dorothy.

"Reasonable? Do you think it's reasonable that people are being killed out there by something no one understands and won't believe? The minute I tell law enforcement to be on the lookout for zombies, I'm through."

"They're not zombies; they're demons," said Rachael.

Burt threw up his hands. "Whatever. People see what they want to see—what they feel they need to see. You have to really believe that we need to find these things, or you never will."

Rhonda scrawled on the map. She looked happy, thriving on newly found purpose, as we all were. We hadn't talked about her leaving, and something told me we may never. Unlike me, she was the type of person who could let things lie.

It's amazing at how far we'd come, from the mental ward to this. We'd weaned ourselves back onto the outside world and found our own way. It felt like we brought some of the insanity inside that place out with us.

Crystal squeezed my hand. "Could we all be enlightened? Is that why the rest of the world is blind to this?"

"Some say there are Buddhist monks that slip in and out of consciousness without even knowing it," said Darren.

"That would explain a lot," I said.

Dorothy shook her head. "If this is enlightenment, I'm not sure how enlightened I want to be."

"I second that," Marie grumbled. "Let me get this straight, we're supposed to track down demons that are out there killing people?"

"Why are you complaining?" asked Darren. "Haven't we been seeking reason all this time? What does it matter, if you're killed by it?"

"K-K-Killed by it?" stuttered Dorothy.

"Give me the choice between death with reason or having no reason at all," said Darren, "and, I'd gladly take up my cross."

"I've been doing this for over six years," said Burt, "and I'm still kicking. Enough talk. We need to get our plan together."

30 FOR THE HOPE OF LIFE

It's difficult when the hopes and answers our loved ones find amount to nothing for us, when they believe so fervently in a greater good that leaves us floating aimlessly in an ocean of ideology.

It is in the quiet times that we realize we're dying. We lounge in monotony and try desperately to believe in something more for ourselves, others and life itself. I cannot explain why at such times death seems so full and life so shallow.

Regardless of what we deserve, the future is a brightly shining beacon. We do not deserve hope, joy or happiness. Yet, our portion exists.

We will be judged if we allow these feelings to drift unused into the cosmos. For life was given by The Great Spirit to live. Failure to experience our share is a slap in the face of God. So live well.

There was a time I expected life to burst forth, a celebratory festival of lights with cherry blossoms floating to earth— something perfect and beyond imagination. A cake so magnificent you don't dare cut it until every last soul is present.

Hope starts as a promise made to yourself, the first drop of rain in a parched land, the first step onto dry earth for a shipwreck survivor. It is a listening crowd for a lonely heart.

What we hope in must be greater than us; therefore, we will always need something greater than man to believe in. Good and evil may be a necessity to perceive our world, but hope is a prerequisite for life.

* * *

By morning, the group was driving in separate directions—each with a map detailing our section of Alaska. I was quiet. My heart felt as though it might ignite. Crystal appeared dazed, resting in the passenger's seat, staring at the world outside the window, her cigarette burning down.

The sun cast a yellow hue on the land, reflecting on the rivers and trees as we drove north toward Point Hope, Alaska.

Things seemed choppy, not quite true, or perhaps so true they were hard to focus on. Our search was like looking through stacks of hay for needles that kept killing the horses. If I'd learned anything though, I'd learned if you don't pursue what's real, it'll track you down. Reality lives both inside and outside of you.

I slid my seat back a notch in an effort to relax. Crystal's leg jumped. She reached to still it, and I took her hand.

She strained a smile. "What are we doing?"

"What do you mean?"

"I mean, are we supposed to kill these things or what? This all seems so crazy."

"We all have demons to face," I said. "I guess it's something each of us has to figure out."

Crystal looked as if she were ready to close her eyes for good. "If it came to it, I don't think I could kill someone, a demon, whatever. Aren't you afraid?"

I leaned over and kissed her. "My greatest fear is losing you."

Instead of mere survival, I was being asked to live with a strength I never knew I had and wish upon a star for something oddly wonderful to happen. Sometimes, the splendid does happen—like the cooling of a fever after sickness—and we aren't surprised by it. Recovery is expected. It's the way life has always been.

Every time I hurt loved ones, it was as though I killed them, but like Jesus, no one really stays dead in a story.

Now that Crystal loved me back, she'd crawled into my cave and was sure to find the horrors within.

She'd come ashore on my island and was sure to be disappointed when, instead of a tropical paradise, there were barren, jagged rocks, few trees, bitter water and cold nights.

My only hope is the dream we all share: that others will discover something in us beyond what we see in ourselves and find sustenance. They will dig for water and build inventive shelters to keep them warm when the winds and rains come.

* * *

The sun burned in the sky, but the earth was cold. We passed a sign that read *Point Hope Population 757*.

A burger joint outside of town stood for civilization. Its red and yellow paint had turned earth tone over the years, melding into a landscape of splotchy evergreens and firs. A gas station leaned into time with the surrounding hillside.

I felt one could easily get lost in the loose grid of streets and scattered houses, though they were few and far between. An occasional yard was adorned with a tricycle or red wagon, but these things seemed as worn as the rest of the town.

I was reminded of Golden Acres, the place I'd lived with Jane and Ashley, and I wondered how many parents here flocked home after work to see their children.

We parked the Buick in front of a white, turn-of-the-century church built with wooden planks. The brisk air smelled of French fries and wildflowers.

A rusty pickup drove slowly past. A young, fair-haired girl sat contently between her mother and father in the cab. I was reminded of Jane, Ashley and the way things could have been. I fought the urge to run and catch the vehicle, throw the man to the ground and drive off with a new, complete family. It could be as easy as that, I thought.

Crystal's leg shook. She grabbed my arm for support. It's so easy to forget about the person leaning on you.

"I hope we find them quick," I said, looking into my wallet. "We don't have the money to stay here long."

Crystal peered up and down Main Street. "How are we supposed to do that?"

We walked to a concrete bunker of a bar with a Budweiser banner decorating its front. Inside was as dark and dank as whale innards. The mouth, a swinging door weighted by sullied flyers.

Crystal and I took seats at the bar and ordered beers from a hefty woman dressed in the plaids of a trucker. She snapped off the caps and set our drinks before us. Down the bar, a black man in a sweat-stained tee-shirt looked into his glass. A wrinkled, nicotine-stained waitress took a deep drag.

A television issued the razz pizzazz of football highlights, a jukebox bellowed ZZ Top's Sharp Dressed Man.

"Are there any jobs in town?" Crystal asked.

The bartender cupped her ear. "What's that?"

"Any jobs . . . in town?"

"Naw, honey." She squinted. "What you see is all there is."

"How many people live here?"

"You mean in town?"

Crystal nodded.

"About seven hundred—says the sign. But all and all, probably less than that. You'd be doing good to move on."

The old waitress cackled from down the bar.

I took a swig—oat and barley alcohol mixed in my mouth. "Anything unusual going on?"

"You mean like people asking about jobs in a town they don't know nothing 'bout?"

I looked up at a used car commercial—a screaming man with a cowboy hat. "Have you been following the murders on television?"

"Insane prick," shouted the waitress in an exhale.

The black man looked up for a moment and then let his head drop.

The news came on after the commercial. The bartender turned it up.

The scene showed Burt Cobbs being helped into the back of a squad car in handcuffs. "Any idea how long this has been going on?" asked a newscaster.

The camera cut to a shot outside Burt's home. Police vehicles lined the drive. Yellow tape sectioned the yard.

A woman with a tame, bleached hairdo and a blue-gray suit stood in front holding a microphone chest high. "Law enforcement is still trying to determine how many people lost their lives in the basement of the house you see behind me.

"For those of you just joining us, I'm standing in front of the home belonging to Yukon-Koyukuk County Sheriff, Burt Cobbs. According to sources 'The bodies of two people were found here this morning by his own deputies along with ten to twelve ice-picks and other weapons.'"

The bartender shook her head. "Sick son of a bitch. Now you can't even trust the cops. . . . 'Nother round?"

I felt like a kite, high above the ground, watching the string that held my unstable nature snap. I floated to where the world was painted with broad strokes of panic.

* * *

Crystal and I parked the Buick outside of town. Water from a nearby stream sounded as though something was coming for us through the forest. I waited for the beast to arrive. I wondered about the others and imagined Burt Cobbs on the other side of steel bars. I wondered which of the others had turned him in.

Crystal pressed her body against me in the half-light of the car. I felt her clawing the sand of my island as she pulled herself onto a long-awaited shore.

I heard the tapping of her feet, climbing the steps of the city she'd managed to build within me. I imagined her on the overlook of a tower, scanning rivers, fields, lakes and mountains for answers that soared like majestic birds.

All of it was both inside and outside, both natural and unnatural, both lies and truth.

I ran my fingers through her hair. "I love you."

She pulled away. "Sheriff Cobbs is evil."

My mind's eye watched a clay pot spiraling with crisp realism toward the rocky floor of my inner chasm.

Crystal thrust a blade into my stomach, softly. Pain disintegrated my vision.

She slid the keys from the ignition and began to cry.

Pain ripped through my stomach in searing waves.

I felt for the knife and the dash and doubled over.

Crystal wailed. "I'm sorry. It's the only way to stop you. You can't see it in yourself. I see your demon!"

She opened the passenger door and disappeared outside. Frigid air filled the car and found its way into me.

I reached for her, but she was gone.

I was alone, searching my soul, wondering where God was.

Birds called out. The stream gurgled. Freezing pain squeezed the life from me.

I closed my eyes and waited and bled.

Then, like so many times before, the voice from the deep spoke and a warm blanket covered my heart.

I wasn't alone.

Crystal believed.

Made in the USA
Charleston, SC
01 October 2013